Out With the Old, In with the Choux

Baker's Rise Mysteries

Book Five

R. A. Hutchins

For the Seed Sowers, the Lawn Mowers,
the Plant Growers…
May your fingers be ever green

CONTENTS

*If you follow this list in order, you will have made a perfect batch of **choux pastries**! In the story, you'll find some delicious suggestions of what to make with your pastry.*

ONE

Flora sank back into her favourite armchair in the sitting room of her little coach house and let out a sigh of happiness. She rotated her ankle gingerly, hoping the day's events hadn't put too much strain on the joint, which had only been free of the cumbersome moon boot for a few days. Finding a stiffness there, but no pain, Flora snuggled the little green bird who sat on her shoulder, enjoying the feeling of his downy feathers nuzzling into her cheek. She had just returned from a lovely day up at the manor house, complete with afternoon tea and not a little wedding planning with her friends. Since Adam's proposal – some seven weeks ago now – the ladies of the village had been keen to bring up the subject at every possible opportunity. Flora didn't mind – she shared their excitement after all – but she and Adam hadn't even set a date yet, so there was still plenty of time for preparations. She had accepted their gushing over her ring – the first time the women had seen it, as Flora had been waiting to get it resized and back from the jeweller's – glad that she had stuck to her guns with Adam and chosen something simple and elegant. Flora's rings from her previous marriage, as chosen by Gregory, had been garish and ostentatious, completely at odds with Flora's own personality. This time, she and Adam had chosen together and Flora sighed with contentment as she looked down at the sparkling emerald surrounded by two small diamonds.

Flora's life had slowed down considerably since her accident, partly because of the limitations naturally imposed on her by her broken ankle, and partly due to her own need to take some time to recover mentally and emotionally from the toll of the past few months. She had therefore temporarily increased Tanya's hours in the tearoom and, after finally receiving her share of the proceeds of the London townhouse that she had once shared with her ex-husband, had offered Amy some part-time hours in the bookshop to fit around her commitments at the salon. Amy, Gareth and Lewis were now living in what had been Billy's house on Cook's Row, and her little baby bump was just beginning to show. If the young woman's wistfulness anytime weddings were mentioned was anything to go by, Flora had a sneaking suspicion that a proposal might be on that couple's horizon before too long.

A buzzing brought Flora's attention back to the present, and she rooted around in her handbag to find her mobile phone. Seeing Adam's number on the screen brought a smile to Flora's lips.

"Flora, love, how did the day go?"

"Hello you, it went well, thanks, very well. The decorators have done a great job in the front sitting room, and the kitchen. They'll move onto the hallway next week and then the study. We'll need to make sure the door to the secret office is firmly closed. The clearance company have almost finished in the attic rooms and will start in the bedrooms next week."

"Did they find anything interesting?"

"Some furniture, old toys, paintings – you can take a look tomorrow, see what you think. They'll take the things we choose not to keep to auction."

"And what about the dining room, have you decided what to do with that space?"

"Not yet. To be honest, the room still spooks me. I can't bear to go in there. All those hunting trophies on the walls. Eugh."

"And what about your time with your friends? Did it relax you at all?" Adam tried to keep the question light and airy, but Flora could detect the underlying concern in his enquiry. He knew more than anyone how the issue of what she was to do with the big house had been weighing on Flora's shoulders, even while she had been at home taking the weight off her ankle.

"Yes, yes, it was lovely. The Victoria sponge cakes I baked in the new range oven up there came out well, even Betty approved! We had a good natter and the gardener came to hand in his signed contract and asked if he could get started right away on some weeding out front. Well, you can imagine how everyone's gaze wandered to the big bay window after that – even Jean's! And her niece who's come to stay from Edinburgh, goodness, her eyes were on sticks!" Adam laughed at Flora's description. He had met Mitch, the new gardener whom Flora had hired at The Rise, once, and he and Flora had both commented then that the lad would likely set hearts racing in the village. He was the definition of tall, dark and handsome. Jean's niece, Phoebe – who was really her great niece, but nobody seemed to bother with the distinction – had seemed particularly enamoured today, often standing up under the pretence of collecting the dirty crockery, when in fact she wandered over to the window and stood looking longingly out. And that despite the reason for her visit being apparently due to needing a break from a complicated love life north of the border!

"Aw I'm glad you had a good time," Adam chuckled, "now I hope you're going to rest this evening?"

"Yes, yes, you know me."

"I do, and that's why I'm reminding you to take it easy! Your ankle is still weak."

"Okay," Flora sighed, but there wasn't much force behind it, "I need to call Lizzie and see how she's getting on with the illustrations for the first Reggie book, but other than that I'll be good, I promise."

"I'm glad to hear it! I'll be there bright and early to pick you up for church tomorrow morning and afterwards we can take a walk up to the manor house while the Sunday lunch is cooking – I've bought everything so I'll bring it across with me. You don't need to lift a finger." Adam ended the call with a declaration of his love for her, and Flora felt the warmth of his words in her chest. She had no doubt that he meant every one of them. Nor did she have any doubt about how lucky she was to be so well cared for.

And it wasn't just Adam – in the past weeks, hardly a day had gone by when Flora didn't have a visit from one of her friends, bringing cake and gossip. Or, in Harry's case, bank accounts and estate forms that required her signature. Their visits had helped her heart but not her waistline, and Flora was very keen to increase her activity again. Especially if a wedding dress might be on her horizon!

After all of the tragedy and trauma surrounding Clarissa Cutter's murder, Flora had almost given up entirely on her aspirations to be a children's author. It was Adam who had suggested that Lizzie – the pet portrait painter – might enjoy the project. Especially since she and Flora got on so well together. Once she thought of it, it seemed an obvious solution and Flora wasn't sure why she hadn't thought of it before. If she could turn back time and never invite Clarissa to the book opening in the first place… anyway, hindsight was a fine thing and Flora knew it was pointless to dwell. She had done too much of that recently.

Too much time on my hands, Flora thought to herself, happy in the knowledge that she was going back to work in the tearoom properly on Monday, and splitting her time between there and the big house.

Whether she sold The Rise, or turned it into a hotel or function venue, all would have implications for the village, and Flora anticipated a rocky time in the near future with some of her neighbours in Baker's Rise. If there was one thing the locals didn't take kindly to, it was change! Shaking the unpleasant thought from her mind, Flora held out her arm for Reggie to jump down from her shoulder to her hand.

"Good bird," Flora said, smiling.

"Good Flora," Reggie repeated, waddling up and down her outstretched fingers. The past weeks had given them the chance to restore Reggie's sense of security and stability – Flora's too, if she was honest – and they had been working on eliminating some of the bird's choice phrases from his repertoire.

"Pleased to meet you," Flora enunciated slowly.

"Please meet you," Reggie chirped back, "Welcome to the tearoom." Flora noticed that he was able to learn a new phrase very quickly now – sometimes even from just hearing it once – and to repeat it back accurately enough to be understood.

"Good bird," Flora brought her hand up to her face and nuzzled her forehead against the soft yellow and green feathers of his little head.

"She's a corker!" Reggie squawked, and Flora couldn't help but smile. Some habits were hard to break! As long as Reggie refrained from being rude to people, Flora was happy to live with his quirks – Besides, if he wasn't quirky, he wouldn't fit so well into Baker's Rise!

TWO

Sunday bloomed with all the beauty of a spring day. April, which was nearly at its end, had been almost free from the showers which often accompanied its name, and Flora wore only a light jacket over her floral dress as she walked to church hand in hand with Adam. The daffodils, which had been in full bloom around the duck pond a couple of weeks ago, had now lost their lustre and only bedraggled stalks remained. This didn't dull the effect of the beautiful scene on Flora's spirit, however, as she always enjoyed this walk through the village. With the church rising before them, and the graveyard surrounding it full of blossom trees which were just beginning to show a hint of their beauty to come, Flora breathed in the fresh air greedily.

"Aw here are the lovebirds," Betty's loud comment could be heard across the Green, from where she stood

9

in conversation with Jean and Mrs. May. Each of the older women wore a pastel coloured hat of simple design, and Flora felt how bare her own head was, just as her cheek's flushed from her friend's comment.

"Chin up, love," Adam whispered into her ear as they approached the group, dropping a swift kiss onto Flora's forehead. Flora tried to pull her hand from his gentle grasp, suddenly embarrassed by the small show of affection, but Adam gave a small shake of his head, "I'm proud to have you beside me, to show everyone how much you mean to me!"

Flora's anxiety calmed at his words. Of course, Betty had meant nothing by the comment, and Flora knew she was probably being overly sensitive. Being in the public eye so much over recent months had caused her to want to protect her privacy – especially regarding her relationship with Adam – with a fierceness sometimes even she couldn't justify.

As if timed to shake off any sombre thoughts, Tanya appeared then coming up from behind to join the couple. Her hat – if so simple a word could be used to describe the flamboyant affair atop her head – was made up of felt chicks and papier-mâché Easter eggs, (despite the event itself having been celebrated a fortnight ago) in a nest made from… *were those actual twigs?* Flora had missed out on seeing this particular creation up till now, as the past two Sundays she had spent at Adam's church in Morpeth as they attempted to integrate their lives further. Never one to not get her full wear out of any outfit or accessory, Tanya appeared to wear the piece with pride though, even crouching down to allow some children a closer look!

If the vicar thought the headpiece amusing, he hid it well, welcoming them all with a smile and a kind word. As if they were waiting for her arrival, his three daughters pounced on Flora before she had even made it through the church porch, "Miss Flora! Miss Flora! Is Reggie with you? Where have you been? Do you have new stories?" Three little voices questioned her at once, and Flora leant down for a group hug.

"Parrots can't come to church," Flora whispered.

"Well, my Daddy works for God, so I'm going to get him to ask him!" Little Evie said with her hands on her hips, never one to be put off by a seemingly unsurmountable obstacle. Adam chuckled as they all trailed behind Betty to their usual pew near the front, admiring the flowers which had been left over from a wedding in the church the previous day.

"Getting any ideas?" Adam whispered once they had sat down and the youngest girl, Megan, had wriggled her way onto Flora's lap.

"About children?" The question came out as a squeak and Flora felt her heart beating wildly in her chest.

"Actually, I was talking about the flowers," Adam gulped audibly and his ears turned a dusky shade of pink.

Thankfully, Betty, who was the only one standing in the aisle and facing the doors at the back, chose that moment to exclaim, "Oh! Ey up!" Her eyebrows were almost in her hairline in shock as everyone turned to see what – or rather who – had warranted that expression. With the cocky arrogance that Flora had detected in him since their first meeting, her new gardener made his way through the throng of gawking locals gathered at the back of the church, Jean's niece on his arm.

"Well, he works fast!" Tanya exclaimed, "Did you know about this Jean?"

"No, the lass told me she was just curling her hair and would be right along. I should have suspected she would pull a stunt like this, after I made her coming to church with me a requirement of her stay," Jean replied, her usually cheerful expression having disappeared to be replaced with one of concern, "I'm grateful for Phoebe's help in the shop, of course, but I fear I may have my work cut out for me keeping her on the straight and narrow the way I promised her mother I would."

"Mr. and Mrs. Miller, Ladies," Mitch tipped his rather old-fashioned cloth cap at them as he and Phoebe took a seat on the other side of the aisle. Flora didn't bother to correct him when he misjudged her and Adam's marital status, preferring not to draw any attention back to herself. She may have hired the man – who looked to be in his mid-to-late twenties – but it was he who had approached her at the beginning of the week, knocking on the door one day when Flora and Adam were up at the manor house to offer his handyman and gardening services. Being in need of just such a person, and thinking it would save her the job of advertising and interviewing, Flora had given his references a cursory glance and then hired him on the spot. Adam hadn't been quite so hasty to trust the lad and had later told Flora that he had secretly run a background check back at the station, but since that had come up clear no more had been said. The newcomer had not asked about any accommodation to do with the role, nor had Flora offered any, so she really had no idea about his life other than he enjoyed taking his t-shirt off while he worked, even on chilly days, as she and all the other women had witnessed yesterday.

Betty had no such reticence in getting information, however, and made a beeline straight for the couple.

"So, when did you two meet?" She directed her question at Phoebe, and judging by the hush which descended in the front half of the chapel, everyone was keen to hear the answer!

"I… well, he happened to pop in to fill his watering can when I was sorting the dishes in the kitchen at the big house yesterday," Phoebe replied, and Flora caught the defensiveness in her voice.

"Oh, to fill his watering can, is that what the young'uns call it nowadays?" Betty cackled at her own joke, and Flora wished Harry were here to temper her friend's curiosity. As it was, the poor man was in home in bed with a heavy cold, and so Betty had no one to rein her in, "You work quick lad!"

Even Mitch had the grace to blush at that, though Phoebe tipped her chin up defiantly as if daring Betty to pass further comment. Never one to back down from a challenge, Betty sucked in her breath until her cheeks were almost hollow, then let out the same breath slowly, followed by a 'tsk, tsk' sound, until eventually she said, "Well, I'm sure your Auntie Jean will tell me all the news, not that it won't be all around the village by teatime anyway!" And with that Betty let out a girlish giggle and hurried to her seat next to Mrs. May as the vicar strode up the aisle and the organ signalled the start of the service.

Keen to rush back to the coach house after the final hymn and put the chicken in the oven to roast for Sunday dinner, Flora promised Betty she would call round on Monday evening to see how Harry was doing, before she and Adam walked quickly up the aisle trying to avoid conversation with her neighbours. Their escape was almost successful, until a stocky man dressed smartly in expensive tweeds stepped out from the last pew to block their path.

"Mrs. Miller, I believe, though I have not yet had the pleasure of making your acquaintance," the man's voice was low and gruff, though it had the distinct accent of the upper classes.

"Oh," Flora took his extended hand and suffered through the rather too strong handshake, "pleased to meet you, Mr..?"

"Errington. Lord Rupert Errington. We have a lot in common, Mrs. Miller, as I own the main estate over by

Witherham, The Withers. I was hoping to have a chat with you, actually…"

"Oh, now isn't exactly a great time," Flora hovered uncomfortably on one leg, trying to take the weight off her still-weak ankle, aware that Lord Errington's hand still rested on hers rather inappropriately and prevented her from moving. Internally, she cursed her very British tendency to remain polite and accommodating, until Adam cleared his throat none to subtly and moved from behind Flora to stand just between her and the man. This forced their new acquaintance to leave his hold on Flora, and she stepped away, closer to the door leading to the church porch and some much-needed fresh air.

The flash of anger on Errington's face was swiftly hidden behind his jovial façade, though not before Flora caught it and it confirmed what her gut had already told her – this was not a man she wished to be better acquainted with.

"Adam Bramble," Adam held out his hand and was met with the briefest of shakes, "we were just in a hurry, actually. Nice to meet you."

And with that, Adam caught up to Flora and rested his hand at the base of her spine, ushering them both out of the building.

"Strange man, gave me the creeps," Flora muttered as they hurried down the path towards the Green as fast as her ankle would allow.

"Indeed," Adam said thoughtfully, though the frown which creased his forehead was soon smoothed away as they chatted companionably. By the time they reached the coach house, their uncomfortable encounter was long forgotten.

THREE

As Adam prepared the vegetables and put the chicken in the oven to roast for their Sunday dinner, which they would have at teatime, Flora quickly changed into some light chinos and a thin top and cardigan ready for their walk up to The Rise.

"And Reggie too! And Reggie too!" her bird squawked as Flora quickly brushed her hair. A phrase that had been taught to him by the Marshall girls, who were always keen for Reggie to feel included in their games when they visited the tearoom and bookshop.

"Yes, yes, good bird," Flora reassured him as she hurried to join Adam in the kitchen.

"All ready, love?" Adam asked, bringing Flora into the circle of his embrace and kissing her tenderly.

"Yes, let's get up there and make some notes on what

the decorators can do this coming week. Then maybe we'll stick our heads into that monstrosity of a dining room."

Adam chuckled and took the tea towel from his shoulder, hanging it neatly on the hook beside the oven, "Okay then, sweetheart, let's go."

With Reggie flying ahead of them, and the afternoon sun giving a surprising amount of warmth for the end of April, Flora and Adam walked up the hill with their arms linked. Entering by the side door as per usual, Flora felt the warmth of her cheery kitchen. She had kept the farmhouse style rather than opting for something more modern and sterile, which wouldn't have been in keeping with the place. Standing at the big kitchen window, overlooking the rose garden which Billy had so cherished, Flora felt Adam's arms come around her waist from behind. Just as she was relaxing back into him, however, Flora felt her fiancé stiffen.

"Stay here love," Adam whispered into her ear, before he slipped quietly back out the way they had come.

"Visitors! Visitors with money!" Reggie shrieked, flying out hot on Adam's heels, his keen eyes having obviously picked out something in the scene which Flora – without her glasses – could not.

19

Torn between following the pair and heeding Adam's advice to stay put, Flora didn't have to deliberate for very long before she saw Adam gesticulating with his arms near the bottom of the rose garden, where a bench identical to Billy and Mabel's was situated. The unmistakable form of her gardener stood from the bench, presumably to respond to Adam's confrontation, and Reggie's distinctive squawk could be heard saying, "You sexy beast!" Flora rushed out of the house and down through the roses, which were just beginning to stir to life.

"Mitch! Adam, he was probably just seeing what needed to be done..." Flora's words died on her lips when she saw who was with the man, trying but failing to subtly rearrange her clothes, "Phoebe! What on earth?"

It was perfectly clear what the pair had been up to, and Flora was furious. Seeing the rage in her eyes, Adam stood back and let her deal with the pair.

"Mrs. Miller, we were just admiring the, ah..." Phoebe stuttered.

"Don't you dare tell me it was the roses! I wasn't born yesterday!" Flora could hear herself shrieking at them, and tried to sound more forbidding than frantic, "This is a breach of trust, Mitch." She turned her steely glare onto the unfortunate gardener, and refused to look away until he did.

"I'm so sorry, really I am, it won't happen again, temporary lapse in judgement," Mitch replaced his cap on his head and stood looking forlornly at his feet. When Phoebe tried to slip her arm through his, he shrugged her off.

The four stood in exceptionally awkward silence for a moment, until Flora said, "I'll see you up here at eight tomorrow morning, Mitch and we'll discuss what needs to be done… in the gardens that is. It goes without saying, that if there is ever a repeat of this… this nature, on my property, then your contract will be terminated."

The young man heaved an audible sigh of relief, nodded his head once quickly and made to leave, just as Phoebe spoke up, "Please say you won't tell my aunt, Flora, I could really do without the lecture."

Flora raised her eyebrows at the request, which was clearly neither an apology nor a sentiment of regret, yet she held her tongue not promising one way or another.

"Perhaps give Flora some time to think it over, eh?" Adam suggested, as Mitch took Phoebe's hand and propelled her down the path which led through the back lawns and then further out to the fields which were part of the estate and ran past Lily and Stan's farm almost to Witherham..

"Well, I never…" Flora exclaimed, catching Adam's eyes just as she saw a flash of mirth there. They both giggled then and that giggle turned into full-blown laughing. It felt good to release the tension, and they walked arm in arm back towards the house.

Their mirth was short-lived, however, when Reggie, who had flown ahead of them, shrieked, "Not that jerk!" from his position perched atop the open side door. Squinting her eyes to see who approached the manor house, Flora spotted Errington just as he rounded the corner.

"No answer from the front, so I just thought I'd come round the back and see if anyone was home," Errington's voice was full of confidence and familiarity, though his expression belied the fact he had not intended to be caught skulking around.

"As I'm sure you know," Flora replied, with no amiable greeting, "I live in the coach house and not up here, so people don't expect to find me here. Always best to make an appointment."

"Indeed," Errington said, though it was almost a sneer and the scorn which he placed on her living somewhere so small when Flora could reside up here in the mansion was palpable even from that one word.

"Stupid git!" Reggie chose that moment to butt into the conversation, no doubt picking up on the tension.

"I didn't realise you had that mangy budgie," Errington screwed up his face in disgust.

Reggie, who couldn't understand the words, but had clearly got the gist of the sentiment, swooped down towards the visitor and landed promptly on his head, digging his claws into the balding, greasy scalp and causing Errington to shout and try to dislodge the creature.

"Reggie, off," Flora said, worried her little friend might get hurt, and pleased when he complied at the first request, "and he's a Double Yellow-Headed Amazon Parrot," Flora added indignantly.

"Reggie clearly recognises you too," Adam said sagely, "been up here a lot, have you?"

Errington looked Adam up and down as if appraising him, "Detective Bramble."

"You've clearly done your homework," Adam's eyes

were mere slits now, his frown a ladder of wrinkles, "And in answer to my question?"

Errington looked as if he would not answer, turning back to face Flora instead, until he finally muttered, "when old Harold was alive, yes."

"Were you and he friends?" Flora asked.

"Friends? Not likely!" Errington's laugh was akin to a bark, and not a very pleasant one at that, "I came around here about once every few months to ask him the same thing I'm going to ask you. Will you sell me the place?"

Flora felt her mouth drop open and knew she must resemble a goldfish, finally managing to whisper past the sudden dryness in her throat, "Wow, that was blunt! The place, as in the whole estate?"

"Yes, manor house, village dwellings, farm, estate lands and of course your own home and that lovely tearoom I spotted. I'm sure I could be accommodating and let you pay me rent to stay on."

"How thoughtful of you," Adam said drily, clearly not wrongfooted by either the man's swaggering arrogance or his imposing stature. Rupert Errington must be six foot six at least, with a girth that was just as impressive. The buttons on his tweed waistcoat were straining across his ample midriff, and even the cool afternoon sun had him sweating profusely.

"I'll think on it," Flora replied, turning back towards the kitchen door and effectively dismissing the man.

"Stinking stranger! More money than sense!" Reggie screeched from her shoulder, a phrase that Flora had never heard and which she assumed had come to his little mind with the memory of Errington's previous visits. Clearly, Harold Baker had not liked the man either.

"I'll come in to discuss it further," Errington said presumptuously, making to follow them.

Adam held his hand across the man's path, and shook his head decisively, "That won't be necessary, not today. Mrs. Miller will be in touch in due course."

And with that, Adam followed Flora into the house, the sounds of Errington's angry blustering being audible until the door was firmly closed and locked behind them.

FOUR

Discussion of Lord Errington's rather brash offer filled Flora's remaining time with Adam that day. So engrossed were they in thinking over the pros and cons of Flora giving up the estate, that before they had even finished the weekly to-do list for The Rise and put on the kettle for a cuppa, the alarm on Adam's phone went off indicating that they needed to get back down to the coach house and take the chicken out of the oven.

The Sunday meal eaten and quick goodbyes said, Adam had to rush off as he was working the night shift on a big case in Newcastle. He promised to run a quick background check on Errington and then he was gone, leaving Flora with a rather empty feeling which she couldn't explain. She had Reggie, of course, so Flora couldn't understand why she felt lonely all of a sudden, especially since she had spent a lot of time recently in her little house with her feathered friend and had not felt as bereft as she did now.

Assuming the day's events had left her a little unsettled, Flora decided to distract herself with a soak in a bubble bath and a glass of red wine. Reggie, too, seemed to approve of this plan, as he chirped from his perch on the back of a kitchen chair as Flora finished drying the last of the dishes.

"My Flora. So cosy," he sang happily, as was his way now when he felt that the door had been closed for the final time that evening and it was just the two of them until the next day.

Imagine his disgruntlement, therefore, when the doorbell rang at that very moment, causing the bird to startle and screech, "Somebody else! Watch out! Hide it all!" in a frantic fashion whilst simultaneously flapping his wings wildly in situ.

"Hush," Flora said, drying her hands and trying to hide the sigh which was eager to slip out, knowing it would only rile the bird up further.

She shuffled along the narrow hallway, her ankle throbbing now after having been on her feet all day, though Flora only just noticed the pain. Peeking out through the spy hole that Adam had insisted she always use now, Flora was relieved to see the familiar face of Sally Marshall.

"Come in!" Flora opened the door to the vicar's wife as enthusiastically as she could muster, sending a prayer of thanks heavenward that it was neither Phil Drayford nor – worse still – Lord Errington on her doorstep.

"Flora, so sorry to bother you. I was hoping to catch you at church, but I was approached by several ladies from the W.I. at the end of the service and then when I looked again you were gone."

"Yes, Adam and I did make a rather speedy exit – or tried to at least," Flora grimaced at the thought of the first of her two encounters that day with Rupert Errington, "come on in."

"Thank you, I promise it won't take long," Sally apologised again as they went into the kitchen and Flora put on the kettle.

Seeing that it was Sally, and not an unexpected male visitor, Reggie puffed up his little chest and put on quite the display, "Welcome to the tearoom!" he said proudly, causing both women to laugh.

"I haven't taught him the words for coach house yet," Flora said, smiling and ruffling Reggie's little head feathers, "tea or coffee?"

"Well, I would ordinarily say tea, but since I'm exhausted and still have the delights of bath and bedtime to get through, I think I need the caffeine!"

"Coffee it is," Flora said, "I think I'll join you."

A cafetière of the proper stuff prepared – which Adam had taken to bringing and leaving for his visits – the two women made themselves comfortable in the small sitting room. Since getting her money from the sale of the marital home in London, and knowing she would be at home for the fitters, Flora had recently had her old windows replaced with double glazed ones which were still in keeping with the old place. Fresh curtains and matching cushions added a pop of lilac colour and, more importantly, the draughts were greatly reduced. With that, combined with the increasing warmth of the season, Flora hadn't needed to light her log burner for the past couple of weeks.

After the vicar's wife had complimented the new soft furnishings and they had chatted about the girls, their discussion turned to the reason for Sally's visit, "Well, Flora, I'm afraid I have a favour to ask of you."

"Ask away, you know I'll do anything I can for the church or the village."

"Of course, though I think this may be stretching it a bit," Sally's frown didn't fill Flora with much reassurance, but she smiled and nodded indicating her friend should go on, "the thing is, the annual baking contest between the Women's Institute groups of our village, Baker's Rise, and that of Witherham is due to take place this coming month."

"And you need a judge?" Flora pre-empted the request.

"Yes, and that's not all, I'm afraid. The contest has been booked in for the third Saturday in May for months now, and there has been much debate as to where it should be held. It's our turn to host, so I automatically assumed we'd use the church hall, but apparently Lady Errington – leader of the Witherham W.I. – has put in an official complaint and said that we need a more neutral venue. Where is more neutral than a house of God, a place of sanctuary and neutrality for centuries...?" Sally stopped to take a breath, looking and sounding exasperated.

"Lady Errington?" Flora went off on a tangent as the name rang alarm bells, "Is she the wife of the Errington who attended church this morning?"

"The very same. Have you met them?"

"Only Lord Errington. Twice today in fact. I can't say that I was particularly enamoured with the man."

"Well, you and me both. Even James, who takes his parish duties very seriously –especially with Witherham's own church having been closed permanently a few years ago as the congregation had dwindled so drastically – doesn't have much time for the couple. Rupert Errington comes around at least once a month, quizzing James on the Baker's Rise estate, how much land it owns and such like. As if James would know! Last time he even offered a donation to the church if James could get him some inside information – the gall of the man! Needless to say, James refused."

This news gave Flora an uncomfortable, unsettled feeling in the pit of her stomach, which must have shown on her face, as Sally rushed on, "I'm so sorry, Flora, you mustn't worry, even if James knew anything about your affairs, he would never divulge…"

"Oh, I know, I know," Flora's voice was barely more than a whisper, "it's just that Errington has made his intentions towards the estate very clear just today actually."

"And what are they?" Sally leaned in closer.

"To buy me out. Completely."

Sally's eyes widened, and Flora fidgeted with the crocheted hem of her cardigan – a gift from Jean during her recent recuperation.

"Well, you aren't thinking about it, are you? The village loves you, we all do!" Sally was incredulous.

"No, no, I don't think so," Flora muttered, though she said it so quickly and judging by the flash of shock which went across Sally's face, Flora knew that her friend wasn't convinced. She didn't even sound convincing to her own ears.

"Of course, it's your decision, Flora, and I can only imagine the amount of work it takes to run such a big venture, what with the tearoom, bookshop, big house and all the rents to manage. Maybe you could take on an assistant or something? Anything rather than that man being in charge. All I hear from the Witherham parishioners is how expensive their rents are and how dilapidated their homes. From what I've heard, it was the same here in Baker's Rise when your predecessor was in charge."

"Yes, sadly it was," Flora let out a deep breath, feeling

the weight of it all on her shoulders, "anyway, sorry I derailed your request. So, you need a judge and a venue?"

"Yes, and well, I think the tearoom will be too small, even if we use both that and the bookshop, so I was wondering if the big house..?" Sally left the question hanging between them. She was obviously uncomfortable making the request, as she ran her hands over her knees, patting out invisible creases in her skirt.

"Too small?" Flora squeaked, "how many will there be?"

"Oh, about two dozen," Sally made a point of staring out of the window then, the expression on her face rather sheepish.

"Well, ah, yes, that should be fine," Flora heard herself say the words, though her spirit shuddered at the thought of so many opinionated women in one place – her place, "the decorators should be completely finished with the downstairs by the time three weeks rolls around."

"Really? Oh thank you so much, Flora!" Sally couldn't contain her gratitude and jumped up to hug Flora affectionately. Sensing the change in mood, Reggie flew across from his perch and hopped up and down on Sally's lap when she sat back down, sharing in her excitement.

"Good news!" he chirped, and both women smiled indulgently as if at a toddler.

"In the grand scheme of things, it's hardly a big request, Sally, please think no more on it. Will you be available to help me set up on the morning?"

"Of course, all the Baker's Rise W.I. ladies will be keen to help I should think – they're determined to give a perfect impression. Oh, and the cakes this year have to be made with choux pastry, eclairs, choux buns and the like."

"Will they be baking them at The Rise?" Flora asked worriedly, thinking of her new range oven which was ample for any domestic needs, but woefully inadequate for two dozen keen bakers all trying to out-bake the next.

"Goodness no! They'll bring their creations," Sally reassured, "I can't tell you how much of a weight off my shoulders this is, Flora."

"Believe me, I understand," Flora said, somewhat subdued.

And she did.

FIVE

Flora tossed and turned so much that night, that even
Reggie had enough of being disturbed by her and took
himself off to his cage in the sitting room with a loud
"Not this again!" Flora was therefore rather tired and
grumpy as she trudged up to the big house to meet
Mitch at eight the next morning. It didn't do much to
improve Flora's temper when the young man was
nowhere to be found at that time, until she saw him
striding over from Billy's old shed which stood in the
corner close to the back of the house, next to the rose
garden.

"I hope you don't mind, Flora, I…"

"Mrs. Miller," it came out even more harshly than
Flora had anticipated, but she said nothing else, simply
raised an eyebrow at the handful of Billy's tools which
Mitch clutched in one hand.

"Mrs. Miller, yes," Mitch began again, though no apology passed his lips, "as I was saying, I had a look in that old shed – which, incidentally, needs tearing down and completely replacing – the lock was rotted away anyway, I'll replace it with one of my own, and I was wondering what the budget is for new tools? This lot look about fifty years past their sell by date."

The man clearly had skin as thick as a rhino's, Flora deduced, given that he had not picked up on the scowl that had adorned her features ever since he started denigrating Billy's prized belongings. Either that, or he was so arrogant as to not care about his new employer's sentiments on the subject. Flora suspected that the latter might well be the case, and the thought worried her.

"Mrs. Miller?" Mitch prompted impatiently, hiding his sigh of exasperation badly behind a fake cough.

"None."

"Excuse me?"

"None. There is no budget for new tools. Those worked for the previous gardener, I'm sure you can make them work for you too," Flora bit out. To be honest, she hadn't even thought about a garden budget other than the gardener's salary, and made a mental note to discuss it with Harry when she saw him that evening. However, she was not inclined to acquiesce to this man's requests right now.

"Well, I, I mean, the rust…"

Flora looked at the tools which Mitch held toward her. They looked old, certainly, but then Billy had been very old and he had still worked well into his nineties. Flora knew that her attachment to her late friend was clouding her judgement. That and the embarrassing scene which she and Adam had interrupted the day before.

"I see no rust," Flora declared resolutely, "and just while we're here, I want to reiterate what I said yesterday. If anything of that sort happens on my property again, I…"

"Yes, I heard you at the time," Mitch interrupted rudely, and Flora bit her tongue hard so as not to give him his marching orders on the spot.

"Very well," Flora turned on her heel, picked up Reggie's carry case from where she could hear him muttering about "that jerk" and "secrets and lies" and strode away to talk to the decorators who had just arrived. She could feel the intense glare of the man behind her, almost scalding her between the shoulder blades, but Flora kept her back ramrod straight and refused to turn around. She was the employer here, and that little upstart would do well to remember it.

The tearoom, in all its cosiness, was a welcome retreat after the tense situation up at the house. The painters, at least, were happy with their own progress and assured Flora they were on track to finish per her schedule. This was the first Monday for several weeks that Flora had been the first to open the tearoom. Normally, she had been coming for just a few hours during the day. This morning, though, she took a moment to savour the peace and quiet, the sun just beginning to peek through the curtains, the daffodils and tulips in vases lovingly displayed by Tanya on every table, and the joy in the everyday and the routine of it all. Reggie, too, seemed to realise that they were starting a new chapter and flew several laps of both the tearoom and bookshop happily, re-asserting his territory before landing on Flora's shoulder and squawking "Welcome to the tearoom!"

"Welcome indeed," Flora replied contentedly, only now taking off her floral jacket and hanging it on the antique coat stand in the bookshop, her heart feeling suddenly lighter than it had in a while. Whatever happened, this little place was hers, it was part of her now, and she would not give it up lightly.

Just as Flora and Tanya were sitting down for a lovely pot of Earl Grey an hour or so later, Lily arrived from the farm shop with the weekly order for the tearoom. Between her carrot cake, various sweet loaves and fruit pies, and Flora's own creations (normally scones, fruit loaf or muffins), the daily order from George Jones the baker had diminished considerably. *Another few months*, Flora thought, *and I will be making enough of my own fresh bakes to be able to cancel that order altogether.* It felt good to be able to plan ahead again, as the black cloud that had settled over Flora following her accident and the whole Clarissa Cutter tragedy was slowly lifting, apart from occasional triggers. Her brain fog seemed to be steadily dissolving too, and thankful Flora was of it.

"Got time for a quick cuppa, Lily?" Flora asked, gesturing to the chair next to her.

Lily gently removed the small bird that had attached himself to her arm and sat down gratefully, "Aye, I think I will, Stan's doing some late season muck spreading on the lower field next to the farmhouse and it stinks something rotten. No matter how long I live as a farmer's wife, I don't think I'll ever like that smell!"

"Eugh, as if all the mud up the legs wasn't bad enough, you're a saint to put up with it, Lily, really," Tanya replied in all earnestness, looking at her high, yellow wedge sandals with a shudder. How she managed to stay upright in them, let alone on her feet all day was beyond Flora. They looked like they were originals from the 70s, so no wonder Tanya shivered at the thought of ruining them. *No one could ever accuse her of being a country lass*, Flora thought amusedly, knowing she wouldn't change her friend for the world.

"So, what's the news?" Lily asked cheerily, pouring herself a cupful from the teapot and adding two sugar lumps, "We didn't make it down to church yesterday as some of the cows are calving and one of them was having a difficult time of it, poor beast. Vet Will was there in his element, he was, giving my Stan a running commentary as if he hasn't been doing it every year for the past thirty years!"

"Well…" Tanya proceeded to fill her in on the gossip about Phoebe and Mitch, and both she and Flora commiserated that their friend had also missed the afternoon tea up at the big house.

"Aye but I'll be there with bells on for the W.I. championship competition in a few weeks," Lily said by way of consolation, "We've got a new farmhand coming to help out, my godson, whose wife can stand in for me in the farm shop occasionally and, more importantly, I've been perfecting a new recipe, all hush hush, and I think I might be onto a winner! That hoity-toity Errington woman won't get a look in this year. Besides we all know she secretly gets a professional French pastry chef to make her entry for her, and then passes it off as her own. It's been the worst kept secret in the Witherham W.I. for the past two decades!"

"Oh really?" Flora's ears perked up at the mention of the woman, "What else do you know about her? Or her husband?" She had tried to pass it off as a nonchalant comment, but Tanya never failed to see through it when Flora was feigning disinterest.

"Got a specific reason for asking?" Tanya looked directly at Flora, her eyebrow cocked. There was no way to put her off when she had her attention trained on you like this. Or, at least, Flora had never found a way! Flora had often thought that Tanya would make a very good detective – blunt speaking and detail-focused.

"Ac-tu-a-lly," Flora drew the word out slowly while she considered how much to tell. In the end she spilled the whole lot about her two meetings with Errington, just stopping short of revealing his designs on the estate. She didn't want to trigger a full-scale local panic. So, instead she glossed over his reasons for wanting to speak with her, hinting only that it was in their roles as estate owners of the neighbouring villages. And instead focused on how uneasy the man made her feel.

"Oh his wife's worse, far worse," Lily declared, not helping Flora's disquiet at all.

"Great, I'm sure she'll be a joy to host up at The Rise," Flora grimaced as Lily stood to leave.

"Aye, she's a nosy one too, that's for sure. She'll be routing around in your drawers if you're not careful! And don't get her started on her supposed charity work. Her latest is taking in her nephew, I believe, though if you heard her you'd think she'd brought in a young child off the streets not a grown man who's her own flesh and blood!" Lily chuckled and they said their goodbyes.

"See you later, alligator," Reggie chanted as Lily reached the door. Flora knew she could thank little Evie Marshall for that one.

"In a while, crocodile," Lily replied, winking at the bird once and then disappearing through the door.

"Is there anything he can't learn to say?" Tanya wondered aloud.

"I don't know if I want to find out," Flora said ruefully, her mind still on the conversation about the Erringtons. Perhaps a visit to The Withers was in order, Flora mused, though the idea struck dread in her. Face the problem head on and take charge of the situation. Be proactive. Yes, that's what she would do. As soon as she could find out what day Betty was free to accompany her!

SIX

The afternoon was drawing to a close, and Amy was tidying the bookshop, Tanya having already left for the day. Flora checked her phone and saw a text message from Sally saying that little Evie had come down with a sickness bug and so she couldn't bring the girls for their usual Monday visit. Flora felt disappointed and worried in equal measure and promised to drop around later in the week with cookies and Reggie to provide entertainment.

"One last cuppa before we close up?" Flora asked, noticing that Amy had grey bags under her eyes and looked exhausted.

"Go on then, I could do with a pick-me-up, truth be told," Amy said, struggling to hide a yawn, "this little one seems to be using all my energy! That and the constant nausea." Amy patted her stomach tenderly.

"Well, I've heard that ginger is good for nausea, and it just so happens there was a ginger and orange loaf in the delivery from Lily this morning. Shall we give it a try?"

"Sounds perfect, thank you Flora," Amy came behind the counter to make the drinks while Flora cut the cake, just as the bell above the tearoom door tinkled and Will arrived, with Shona and Aaron following close behind.

"Perfect timing!" Flora declared, shouting over Reggie who had become very loud and animated on seeing his little friend Aaron, "We were just going to have tea and cake."

"Grand, thanks Flora," Will seemed a little out of sorts, his face already a subtle shade of pink with the blush spreading from his ears to his cheeks.

Interesting, Flora thought as she watched how he pulled Shona's chair out for her in a gentlemanly fashion and then took Aaron into the bookshop to find some colouring.

"Do you mind if we sit with you?" Amy asked Shona, carrying across a large pot of Earl Grey.

"Not at all, I've got some news, actually," Shona said,

beaming from ear to ear and waving her left hand around conspicuously.

"Shona, is that a new ring I spy?" Flora asked, bringing five slices of ginger loaf on a large tea plate and taking a seat next to the women.

"It might be," Shona said coyly, just as Will came from the other room to join them.

"Tell us!" Flora urged, sure that what she had spotted was an engagement ring.

"Well, yes, Will has proposed and I said yes!" Shona gushed, holding her hand out for them to admire as Will cleared his throat a few times and sat down. His face was flaming red now and whilst he seemed extremely happy, Flora understood that he felt uncomfortable being the centre of attention.

Flora and Amy oohed and aahed, examining the ring from different angles under the light. If Amy was a little quiet and subdued, no one other than Flora noticed as Shona began regaling them with the proposal details, from the sunset walk to the rose petals and champagne.

"So romantic!" Flora sighed, "Will, you did a great job."

"Aye, well I, ah, long overdue, been meaning to for a while, ah," Will couldn't seem to get his words out in a straight line, and Shona took his hand in hers on the tabletop, "thanks, ah, yes had to wait till calving was nearly done. Don't want to propose when you've had your hand up a cow's behi…"

"Anyway," Shona cut him off before he could launch into one of his favourite topics of conversation – the bovine birth canal – one she had heard plenty of times before, Flora was sure.

Reggie came to perch on the table, hoovering up the scraps of loaf that were left. Flora knew it was unhygienic and had she not been sitting with friends she would never have allowed it. As it was, she tried to shoo the enthusiastic parrot away, but he refused to budge until every last crumb was gone.

"Ah, Flora," Will spoke from behind his china teacup.

"Yes?"

"Isn't Reggie a bit, well, larger than the last time I saw him?"

Flora felt the heat rise up her neck. It was true that the vet hadn't seen Reggie for a while, given that Flora and her feathered friend had spent a lot of time at the coach house recently. It was also true that Reggie seemed somewhat heavier when he sat on her hand, as he had finally decided to do now. If she was being honest, Flora knew that they both wore the effects of little exercise and a lot of comfort snacking. She said none of this however, simply raising her eyebrows at Will and giving a half smile.

"Will, don't be rude!" Shona interjected.

"I'm a vet, I notice these things," Will spoke in his own defence, encouraging Reggie to jump onto his own arm where he could examine him more closely, "Aye, little fella, what you need is a diet! No more fruit salads, no more midnight bowls of sunflower seeds."

How he had known their secrets, Flora didn't care – she felt called out, but the evidence spoke for itself and she could hardly argue.

"I can get a plan drawn up for you," Will offered kindly.

"Yes, thanks," Flora whispered, wondering who would draw up a similar plan for herself.

Whilst Reggie didn't understand the word 'diet' nor any of the conversation really, he knew they were talking about him and sat preening his feathers happily on Will's arm. *Poor little thing,* Flora thought to herself, *he has no idea that the fruit train's been shut down.*

When the little family had left, and Amy was gathering her things to leave, Flora put a gentle hand on her shoulder, "You know, Amy, when I was younger and married, every time I saw a pregnant woman I felt jealous. I'm not saying I'm jealous of you, of course. Just that, sometimes when we see people who have got the thing we long for, then it can bring up feelings of a green eyed monster that we really wish would just stay in its hole. We can't control our envy sometimes, and that's human."

Amy nodded slowly, and Flora was horrified to see tears running down the younger woman's face.

"Oh Amy, oh my goodness, I didn't mean to upset you! I wanted you to know your feelings are natural, that I understand about how you feel when you see other couples getting engaged. Oh my goodness, I…"

"Flora, please, pay me no heed, it's the pregnancy hormones. I'm always blubbering," Amy looked just as embarrassed as Flora felt, and Flora really wished she had kept her mouth firmly closed.

Sensing the tension in the air, Reggie flew to Amy's shoulder and chirped, "She's a corker," causing the woman to smile and rub her wet cheek against his soft feathers.

"Apparently, you're a better judge of social situations than I am," Flora whispered to her little feathered friend after they had waved Amy goodbye. She herself felt absolutely mortified and knew she would need to tell Adam about her huge faux pas, just to get it off her chest.

Closing up her little empire for the night, Flora was looking forward to dropping Reggie off at the coach house and then going straight down to visit Betty and Harry. She hoped Harry was recovering from his head cold and that the couple could distract her as they usually did with their inside knowledge of local affairs and Betty's homemade Victoria sponge. The thought of cake caused Flora to run her hands absentmindedly over her hips as she took off her apron. Perhaps just half a slice…

SEVEN

The evenings were lighter and warmer now, so the walk down to Betty's cottage was a pleasant one and Flora felt a lightness in her step at the thought of spending time with her friends. Her contentment was short-lived, however, when Betty only opened the door after Flora had rung the bell three times, the older woman looking tired and drawn.

"Aw Flora lass, I fair forgot you were coming round, come in," Betty walked with a slower gait than normal, her back slightly hunched. All of the energy seemed to have been sucked from her body, even since the previous day at church.

"Betty, what is it?" Flora asked as soon as they were in the kitchen where Betty was filling the kettle, seemingly acting more on autopilot than anything else.

"Eh?" It was like Betty suddenly became aware of Flora's presence again.

Flora had never seen her friend so out of sorts, "Do you have the virus? The cold? From Harry?" Flora asked gently.

"Nay lass, I'm fit as a fiddle, just tired. I've been up the past few nights with him, kept awake by his coughing and worrying about the man, but last night was by far the worst."

"You should have called me, Betty, I would have stayed the night and helped you out. Has the doctor been round?"

"Aye, Doc Edwards came this afternoon. Says it's gone onto Harry's chest. I could have told him as much myself. Pah! Anyway, he says we have to keep an eye out that it doesn't get any worse," her eyes were unusually glassy.

"Where is Harry now? Can I see him?"

"He's in bed, lass, where he's been for nearly a week now," Betty's voice faltered, and a sharp look of pain and worry passed across her face before she could school her features into composure once again.

"Aw, come and let me get you sat down in the sitting

room with a cuppa, then I'll pop my head in on him," Flora said softly, putting her arm around Betty's shoulders and noticing how frail her friend seemed. Even little Tina the Terrier was lying beside the unlit hearth, keeping quiet and out of the way, which was very out of character. It was like a grief had already settled over the tiny cottage, and Flora had to physically shake herself in the kitchen to get rid of the unwanted feeling.

After preparing a cup of chamomile tea for Betty and a breakfast blend for Harry, Flora tiptoed to the main bedroom with the china cup and saucer on a tray with two custard cream biscuits. No response came when Flora knocked the first time, so she knocked again until she heard a hoarse voice hidden behind a wracking cough telling her to come in. Nothing could have prepared her for the sight of Harry lying in bed, propped up by several pillows, his face grey and taut.

Flora swallowed the gasp that rushed up her throat and plastered a smile on her face, "Just brought you a hot drink and some biscuits, Harry. If I'd known how, er, how you were doing I would have been round sooner."

"Nay lass, tis just a cold, and you've plenty of things to be doing and remembering," the effort of speaking caused another bout of coughing and Flora felt her eyes fill with unwanted tears as Harry patted her hand in a fatherly fashion.

Flora set the tea and biscuits on the bedside table and hovered awkwardly, half of her wanting to leave the room in case her errant emotions caught up on her – Flora didn't want to upset Harry by crying in front of him. The other half of her wanted to perch on the end of the bed and talk to him, to listen to his sage words, selfishly knowing that he would be the one to know what to do about Errington's offer.

As if reading her mind, Harry pointed to a chair in the corner of the room which Flora hadn't seen, "Grab that seat, lass, and come and talk to me for a minute," Harry gasped out the words, his breaths coming short and shallow.

"Harry, I think we should get you checked out at the hospital. Please," Flora said, not above begging when it came to her friend's health.

"Have you been listening to Betty?" Harry asked, coughing when he tried to laugh a little.

"No, no I would just feel better if we got a second opinion," Flora began, but was interrupted when Harry placed a light hand on her knee.

"Flora lass, pass me the water."

"Of course, of course, sorry," Flora helped him to take a small sip, before sitting back down next to the bed.

"Listen carefully, lass, and don't interrupt," Flora strained her ear to hear Harry clearly, "I want you to know that..." More coughing, another sip of water.

"Harry, can't we talk another time, when you're feeling better?" Flora felt her hold on her emotions slipping as Harry forced himself to continue.

"Nay lass," he spoke more forcefully now, gripping her arm for emphasis, "I need you to know how proud I am of what you have done since you came here. You're fair and honest, you've turned this village around."

"Well, I don't think..." Flora couldn't speak around the lump in her throat.

"Selfishly, lass, it does my heart good to know that Betty is safe in this little cottage, that you won't try to raise her rent when I'm gone," Harry sank back against the pillows, overcome with the exertion of speaking.

"Gone?" Flora squeaked, "No Harry, you're not going anywhere! Except maybe to hospital. And of course, I wouldn't even charge Betty any rent if you hadn't insisted on it all being equal and above board for everyone in the village. It is you who showed me how to run this place, who was the first to welcome me, who has been like a father…" the tears flowed then, and it was as if the dam had broken. Flora sobbed openly and Harry patted her arm softly, until his hand slipped away as he succumbed to sleep.

Flora leant down to check that he was still breathing before taking a moment to try to compose herself before returning to Betty. For once, Betty made no comment on Flora's obvious distress, understanding immediately what had caused it, and simply indicated a seat on the sofa.

"Betty," Flora began when she felt she could trust her voice again, "I'll be back in the morning, and we'll drive Harry to the hospital. If he goes downhill overnight you call 999. Okay? Promise me, please."

"Aye lass," Betty whispered, her own lip trembling. Little Tina jumped up onto Betty's lap and the older woman stroked the dog's back absentmindedly. They sat in silence for a few minutes, until Flora rose to hug her friend and then left quietly, making sure the door was locked behind her as she went.

As if they had a mind of their own, Flora's feet turned right out of Betty's cottage instead of left and headed straight down to Jean's shop. She desperately needed to speak to someone, someone who knew Betty and Harry even better than she did. If she was honest with herself, Flora needed a mother figure to reassure her that Harry would be okay. She felt pathetic even admitting it to herself, but then decided that perhaps there was strength in leaning on friends in times of need, and it wasn't the weakness that her instinct told her it was. Her own parents had been very insular, without a circle of close confidants, happy in each other's company. Then Gregory had always had friends who performed a function in his life – golf buddy, drinking partner and so on, always on a purely superficial level – and so Flora had spent most of her marriage feeling exceptionally lonely.

Here though, in Baker's Rise, she had a community, a literal village to support her, and Flora was so thankful for it. They had come together to grieve for their own in recent months, and they would come together to help Betty and Harry now. An idea formed in Flora's mind – she would ask Jean to help her make a plan of action, people who could cook meals for the couple, take turns walking Tina, and pop in to check on the pair.

At the same time, another decision solidified in Flora's heart. Whatever she was offered, she was certain now that she wouldn't give up the estate. It had come to her for a reason, and whilst she was in a position to do so Flora would use her position to help as many people as possible.

EIGHT

Emboldened by her new resolve, Flora had phoned Lord Errington then and there on the street to arrange a meeting at The Withers for the following afternoon, not caring that she would have to attend the appointment alone. Then she had spent a good half hour with Jean, formulating a plan to support Betty and Harry. Finally, and rather on impulse, Flora had called in on Doctor and Mrs. Edwards, forcing herself to walk quickly to their address before her nerve failed her. She had never been to their home before – and would not have done so now had the visit not been born of necessity – and Flora faked her best 'lady of the manor' posture as she waited nervously for the front door to open.

"Apologies for the lateness of the hour," Flora said

quickly as Edwina Edwards stood on the mat with an expression halfway between annoyance and surprise. The normally abrasive woman must have quickly remembered the curlers in her hair, as she patted her head self-consciously and invited Flora inside, where Doctor Edwards sat in the immaculate and rather sterile sitting room, reading the local newspaper, and smoking an old fashioned tobacco pipe.

"Ah, Mrs. Miller," he coughed and spluttered, trying to hide the smoking implement behind the newspaper, "apologies, disgusting habit I can't seem to break."

It was the first time that Flora had heard the good doctor speaking as a normal person and admitting a weakness, and she smiled in acknowledgement of that fact, "we all have our guilty pleasures, doctor, and if not in our own home, then where else can we truly be ourselves?"

"Where indeed," the doctor folded his newspaper in four equal quarters and gave Flora his full attention.

"Please, do sit down," Edwina reappeared, the curlers having disappeared, "I'll make some tea."

Almost wrongfooted by the hospitable welcome, Flora sat down awkwardly, as if she was waiting for the other shoe to drop.

"How can we help you?" Doctor Edwards asked, clearly waiting for Flora to begin.

"Well, I understand you saw Harry Bentley this afternoon. I know you cannot break patient confidentiality, but I have just been there and he seems to be much worse than just having a cold and possible chest infection."

A flash of annoyance passed over the doctor's features, and Flora knew he would hate to have his judgement questioned, but she ploughed on regardless, "I will be taking him to the hospital tomorrow morning if he is no better."

"Well, Mrs. Miller, I was not aware you had medical training," the doctor stated brusquely, before seemingly catching himself and then backtracking, "my apologies, it has been a long day. I listened to Mr. Bentley's chest and was not overly concerned, though I'll admit it was hard to hear much of anything in his chest cavity what with Betty's incessant anxious chatter and the constant coughing. I will return there now and check on him."

   "Oh! Really? Thank you so much," Flora stood at the same time as the doctor and watched as he retrieved his medical bag from a corner of the adjoining dining room. She had not expected him to acquiesce so easily, and ended up hurrying in his wake as he called through to Edwina that tea was not required and then left the house.

Flora kept Betty out of the bedroom when the doctor examined Harry for the second time that day, trying to reassure her verbally and when that didn't work, asking for some advice with a recipe for miniature carrot cakes. That sparked the older woman's interest and filled the time until Doctor Edwards reappeared, his expression sombre.

"Well doctor, what do you think? He's a stubborn old goat that's for sure, but he's my old goat and I…" Betty launched herself into another speech, clutching her hands nervously.

"Shh, Betty, let him speak," Flora whispered, putting her arm around her friend's shoulders and finding her shaking.

"Well, you were correct to fetch me, Mrs. Miller," Doctor Edwards exhaled sharply, "Mr. Bentley has indeed gone downhill rapidly since I saw him last and I have called for an ambulance to take him to hospital, where they can better check his lungs and monitor his breathing."

"No!" Betty's legs almost buckled under her, and had

Flora not already been so close and in a position to catch the woman, then she would certainly have ended up on the floor.

"Come now, Betty, sit down in the armchair and I'll fetch your coat and shoes," Flora said, as the doctor returned to Harry's bedside, "you'll be wanting to go with the ambulance. I'll hurry back to the coach house when you all leave, and then follow you in my car. You won't be alone, I promise."

"Such a good lass," Betty stroked Flora's hair, where she kneeled beside her chair and Flora tried to swallow the lump in her throat. Now was a time to be strong. For Betty and for Harry.

Flora's whole body felt the effect of spending most of the night at the specialist hospital in Cramlington. Despite Betty's protests that Flora should get home and to her bed, Flora had of course stayed with her friends for as long as possible, eventually getting home at four in the morning. The hospital doctors were still running tests, but it was suspected that Harry had pneumonia and so he had been moved to a ward. Of course, Betty had refused to leave his side and Flora was due to meet Adam there later once she had kept this stupid appointment at the Withers. She wanted to quash any speculation that she might sell The Rise, and make it quite clear to Errington that any moves on his part in that direction would be futile. Then Flora would collect some things for Harry and fresh clothes for Betty too, before returning to the hospital.

The thought of the confrontation had given Flora so many nerves that she had even skipped lunch, considering it a win for her new diet. Reggie had been less pleased, however, both with the lack of his usual morning round of three breakfasts – just a few measly grapes had been on offer - and with the new handwritten signs that Flora had placed inconspicuously on the tables in the tearoom, stating, 'Please do not feed the parrot.' Of course, Reggie could not read, but it had only taken a couple of customers who would normally feed him their crumbs shaking their heads sadly and pointing to the new signage, and the clever bird had worked out what that meant for him – the end of all-day snacking. In a fit of pique, the cheeky parrot had swooped at the offending signs whenever Tanya and Flora had their backs turned, flinging them to the floor with his beak. Just before she was due to leave for her appointment, Flora had even felt one of the little missiles hitting the back of her head. Reggie seemed to realise he had gone too far then, and flew straight back to his perch, hiding his head under a wing.

"Don't think you can do that and get away with it! Bad bird!" Flora stood with her hands on her hips, her chest heaving with indignation. It was only Tanya's chuckle from behind the counter that made Flora realise how silly she was being, scolding the bird in such a manner,

"Save your feistiness for Lord Errington," Tanya counselled, "he will be a much better target!"

Of course, she was right, and Flora headed back to the coach house with her sulking pet to change into one of her 'power suits' for her dreaded visit to The Withers.

NINE

Flora's car had not been right since it had crashed into a ditch the night she broke her ankle. In fact, Flora feared that neither the car nor the ankle would be the same again. The rather elderly vehicle had been fixed, of course, but it rattled more than before and occasionally appeared to be on the brink of overheating. Since Flora normally only did very short trips around the local area, she didn't really pay it much heed, but the journey back from the hospital in the early hours of the morning had been a different matter and, rattled in more ways than one, Flora had phoned a garage to take a look. The earliest they could fit her in was the following week, and as they were the only mechanics for miles, Flora could do nothing else but wait. Besides, she would need her car to travel to and from the hospital for the foreseeable future.

So it was, that she turned onto the long driveway which led up to The Withers, her car chugging and puffing like an old coal-fired steam engine. Not exactly the entrance Flora had hoped to make, but she ploughed on regardless. That was, until the thing broke down completely about a third of the way along the tree-lined route. Unlike The Rise, the Withers was on a flat piece of land, and for this Flora was relieved, as it meant she had no hill to climb. Grabbing her handbag from the back seat – a beautiful Italian leather creation in soft lilac, which matched her kitten-heeled slingbacks – she began the rest of the journey on foot.

What had seemed like a very manageable distance by car, had turned out to be a deceptively long walk. One of Flora's heels gave up when she was almost at the manor house, snapping with an alarming crack that caused her to go over on her other ankle. Now she had two throbbing ankles, and was absolutely baking in her wool suit jacket. Throwing the jacket over her shoulder and loosening the top two buttons of her smart blouse, Flora gritted her teeth, determined to make it to the imposing double front doors of the manor house.

Is it a hot flush, the weather, or that I'm exceptionally unfit? Flora wondered morosely as she limped the last few meters up to a decidedly ornate fountain which stood in the middle of the gravelled courtyard at the front of the building. Feeling the sweat trickling down her brow and into her eyes, Flora leaned over the stone sculpture and scooped some water from the hands of a rather grim looking cherub, lapping it up from her own palms greedily and then even going so far as to splash some over her face. Bent over and hidden by the bulk of the fountain as she was, Flora didn't see the two men who strode around from the side of the building, and nor did they spot her, but she could certainly hear their voices raised in agitation.

"It's not enough! Not enough at all!" Errington's posh rasp could clearly be heard as the men approached.

"I realise that, but these things take ti..," the conversation stopped abruptly as the men found Flora, who was deliberately hiding behind the stonework of the decidedly ugly central mermaid now.

"Mrs. Miller, I thought our meeting was half an hour ago?" Errington did a slight double take as Flora stood to her full height, tottering off balance on her one good shoe. His eyes swept the full length of her, and the man clearly couldn't hide the look of disgust which adorned his features for the few seconds before he managed to school them into something more gentlemanly, "You, ah, walked? From the village?"

Ignoring his contemptuous tone and his rude appraisal of her outward appearance, Flora squared her shoulders, ran her hand once over hair, which was wet and plastered to her forehead, and replied, "My car decided to have a moment. It is back there, on your driveway." That the other man was her new gardener, Mitch, was not lost on Flora and she was about to ask how the two men knew each other, when the younger of the two spoke up.

"Mrs. Miller, I was just finishing up some work here at The Withers, so that I can focus completely on your gardens up at The Rise. I was hoping to speak with you actually. Would you care to ride back with me in my truck?"

"I, well, I," Flora realised she did not have many options, "if you could wait until I have spoken with Mr…ah, Lord… Errington then that would be kind, thank you."

At least she had not lost her manners, Flora thought to herself, levelling her gaze at Errington and refusing to shrivel under his blatant assessment of her present state.

"Well then, would you like to come inside, Mrs. Miller, and have some, ah, proper refreshment?" Errington watched as Flora tried to surreptitiously dry her hands on her suit trousers.

Flora nodded once and followed him, limping on one shoe with a heel and one without, to the large, wooden doors, whilst Mitch hurried back around the side of the building. To say the receptions rooms were grand was an understatement. First a large hall, with garish faux-gold cherub statues perched on tall marble columns greeted them, then they passed a huge, almost-empty room on the left with a parquet floor and furniture only around the sides of the space – *a ballroom?* Flora wondered – before entering a drawing room that looked like it could be the set for a performance of 'Antony and Cleopatra'. The Roman theme continued, with more marble, low chaise-longues, cherubs in various positions, and a large internal fountain – *yes, that is indeed a fountain,* Flora stared in horrified awe – which was the centrepiece of the space. If Flora had hoped to get some inspiration for her own manor house decor, then she would have been sorely disappointed. Garish and vulgar were the first two adjectives which sprang to her mind.

The relaxing sound of trickling water was soon drowned out by a cacophony of barking and a tall, broad woman swept into the room from a door in the opposite corner to the one in which they now stood, looking imposing in knee-length riding boots, jodhpurs and a riding jacket. Following behind her, in a long line that looked like a trail of ants and made Flora want to giggle, were at least eight little dogs. Maltese terriers, Flora knew them to be, as Betty had once given her an in-depth lecture on the different types of terrier, when Flora had mistakenly called Tina a Yorkshire terrier, when she was in fact a Norwich terrier. Their fur was long and brushed to perfection, stopping just at floor length so as to hide their little legs completely, thus giving them the air of floating along, and each had a different coloured bow keeping their fur from falling into their eyes.

"The position has been filled," the woman spoke as she approached Flora, her nose wrinkling at what must surely be a disgusting sight, if the expression on her face was anything to go by. Not her forehead though. No, that appeared to have been botox'd into submission and was as smooth as the marble statues which surrounded them. It was the woman's beady eyes which scrunched up and peered at Flora as if she were sullying the space by simply being there. Eyes which reminded Flora distinctly of Detective Blackett. When the woman stopped abruptly, the dog behind her was caught unawares and it was like a row of dominoes bumping one into the other and ruining the previous graceful effect. Had she been in any other company, Flora would have laughed out loud.

"Which position?" Flora couldn't help but bite back.

"The one for cleaner, of course, I presume that is why you are here."

Errington coughed uncomfortably, "Ah dear, let me introduce you to Mrs. Flora Miller, of Baker's Rise."

"This is her? The one you want to buy out? Oh, you've got it in the bag, darling," the woman giggled girlishly – a rather distasteful sound to Flora – and swept past them both, her little train of terriers gliding behind like a long, furry caterpillar.

"Enjoy your ride," Flora said, in her most sarcastic tone.

"Oh, I don't ride," Lady Errington shot back, "but one has to look the part. Something you have clearly not learned!"

Before Flora could think up a suitable retort that didn't include one of Reggie's favourite inappropriate phrases, the woman had gone from the room and the sound of trickling water could be heard again, reminding Flora that she really could do with using the bathroom.

TEN

Well, that was a waste of time, Flora thought to herself, as she refused Mitch's offer of help and instead hoisted herself into his dirt-covered truck in a most ungainly fashion. To say that was simply an understatement, would be to ignore the true reality of what had transpired back in the house. When Flora, having refused the offer of refreshments, had spoken her piece, stating in no uncertain terms that she would not be persuaded to sell The Rise or any of the accompanying estate, Errington had laughed. Yes, laughed. Worse than that, he had guffawed for a good few minutes, his large belly shaking beneath his over-stretched golf jumper.

"Whatever you say, Mrs. Miller," he had finally managed to reply, through tears of mirth which rolled in fat droplets down his cheeks, "Goodness, if I'd known you did comedy, we could book you for one of Lavinia's dinners!"

"Well, I..." Flora had been lost for words, and so she had left. Rather abruptly, with an absurd limping gait, and with a childish stomp of the foot for good measure. Luckily, Mitch had already pulled the truck around the front, and so here she now sat, fuming and in pain – as much from her wounded pride as her dodgy ankles.

The silence was palpable, and stretched uncomfortably between them, until Mitch eventually said, "I took the liberty of asking a friend to come and look at your car, Mrs. Miller. He should be here in the next hour and if he can fix it today then I'll have it back to you this evening."

"Really?" Flora felt the embarrassing swell of emotion which warned that tears were imminent and tried desperately to control herself, swallowing several times before continuing, "That is very kind thank you. I'll give you the keys. Let me know how much I owe you when he's seen the problem."

"Well, ah, the thing is, Mrs. Miller..."

"You can call me Flora if you like," she offered, feeling mollified towards the young man.

"Thank you, Flora, I was hoping for a favour actually."

"If it's putting in a good word for you with Phoebe's great aunt, then…"

"No! No, nothing like that, it's just that I've found myself unexpectedly, ah, without accommodation, and I was wondering if there's a spare room up at The Rise?"

Flora disguised her surprise by repositioning her handbag on her knee as she thought about her reply. At length, she said, "I could have one of the box rooms cleared, there is a small one at the back overlooking the gardens which shouldn't take the clearance company long to sort. I'm afraid it's in dire need of re-decoration…"

"Yes, yes that would be perfect. Just a temporary stop-gap until I find somewhere more permanent. I will pay you rent of course."

"Well, we'll work that out, yes. As you know I don't live there, so you can use the kitchen and keep your food in the fridge and cupboards. The plumbing is new, though the baths themselves look like they were past their best by the 1950s…"

"Really, Mrs. Mi…, ah Flora, I'm very grateful, none of

that stuff bothers me."

"Very well, I'll get you a key from Mr. Bentley," Flora's stomach dropped as she remembered that poor Harry was currently lying in a hospital bed, "Ah, I'll get a key to you tomorrow and you can move in straight away."

"Thank you, Flora, thank you so much."

The man seemed so genuinely grateful, that Flora felt herself blush. *Besides*, she thought to herself, *perhaps it would be good to have someone living up there, to keep an eye on things.*

"Ack! My Flora! Ack!" Reggie shrieked in her face as Flora entered the coach house. Catching sight of herself in the small hallway mirror, Flora was inclined to agree with him. She was horrified at her own appearance, but it was too late to rewind the day now. Too late to redo her conversation with Errington. The whole embarrassing encounter would be forever etched in Flora's memory. Her only consoling thought was that she was under no obligation to sell to the odious man. Or to anyone for that matter. He could bluster and bark, persuade and cajole until the cows came home, but Flora was determined she would not budge.

A hot shower, fresh clothes and a cup of strong coffee and Flora was feeling somewhat rejuvenated. Even Adam calling to tell her that he had to work late on the difficult case he was investigating did not dull her mood. Flora was determined to visit the hospital in a positive and confident frame of mind. Her car was returned to her just before six o'clock that evening, with Mitch refusing to take any money for the repairs. Flora therefore offered to waive his first fortnight's rent and they both seemed pleased by the outcome.

Just as she was about to leave the coach house to drive to visit Harry, her mobile phone rang and Betty's number showed on the screen. The older woman had only recently begun carrying the phone with her, encouraged by Harry, though she only used it when she absolutely had to, and then only for calls, never texts or to browse the internet.

"Betty? How are you?" Flora asked, her stomach lurching at the unexpected communication.

"Flora lass, it's Harry, they've had to put him in an ind.. ind..ucted coma."

"An induced coma? Oh no," Flora's intention to remain positive disappeared as quickly as it had come.

"Aye lass, so they can annihilate his lungs, so they

say."

"Annihilate? Maybe you mean ventilate?" Flora asked gently, "Put him on ventilation to give his lungs a break. You must be so tired, Betty, let me come and collect you. Maybe Harry isn't aware you're there while he's sleeping."

"No, no, he knows. I'm staying."

"Come back to the coach house with me, or I'll bring Reggie and we'll stay with you. Let's get you some food and sleep and I'll take you back in the morning." Flora was not prepared to take no for an answer, "I'm leaving to come and get you now."

Betty clicked her tongue in disagreement but said nothing other than a very quiet, "See you soon then."

Flora grabbed her bag, some overnight things, and finally put Reggie in his carry cage, "Too late! Cosy now!" Reggie squawked, protesting the unexpected evening adventure.

"Good bird," Flora whispered on repeat, taking comfort from having her little friend with her. Nothing mattered now – not big houses or eccentric gentry or gardeners – nothing except her friends and getting Harry better.

ELEVEN

Two weeks. Two long weeks had passed since Harry had been put on the ventilator that was helping him to breathe and keeping him alive. Two weeks that Flora had been living at Betty's and co-ordinating the support efforts along with Jean. All of the villagers had played their part, whether visiting Harry, driving Betty to the hospital, or keeping her company and distracted while Flora worked.

To be honest, Flora no longer knew whether she was coming or going. Since neither she nor Betty had had much appetite, she had started to notice her clothes feeling looser, though her body itself felt heavier. The worry, the exhaustion, had taken their toll. Even Reggie was much more subdued, and no longer protested his simple two meals a day, though he often spread out his eating of those two bowlfuls over the course of the day and evening.

With poor Harry out for the count and Adam rushed off his feet with the biggest investigation he had ever taken part in – a serial killer on the loose in Newcastle-upon-Tyne – Flora had had to stand firmly on her own two feet. She had made all of the decisions pertaining to the manor house and had dealt with all of the small problems which arose – of which there had been a worrying number.

It had begun with a couple of smashed windows down in the laundry room behind the kitchen, and a hooded figure showing on the security cameras at the side of the building. Then, a few nights later, someone had painted graffiti on the front wall of the manor, also smashing the flower boxes which hung underneath the big bay windows. Unfortunately all when Mitch had been out for a meal in Alnwick with Phoebe. The locks had been changed just in case, the wall power washed, only for a fire to start outside the following week. Billy's old shed had burnt to the ground, and all his vintage tools destroyed. Even Mitch had seemed upset at that, and Flora had quickly bought him a brand new shed and a whole range of tools to put in it. He had added a thick padlock and two bolts for good measure.

Flora didn't know what she would have done without the young man. He had proved to have a steady head on his shoulders and, other than some strange habits such as needing his space precisely ordered and pristine, he had been practical and thoughtful in his help, ingratiating himself into Flora's good favour. Flora had thought it odd that he had put a lock on his tiny room, and even gone so far as to labelling his shelves in the fridge and cupboards. With the spate of petty crime targeting the manor house, she didn't blame him for keeping his things locked up, but she did think the whole kitchen thing was going a bit too far. For once, though, Flora had managed to keep her errant tongue in check, and the pair had worked together to co-ordinate the window fitters, the decorators and room clearance team. Adam had been worried about the unusual activity, and wanted to do more, but his hands were currently tied with all the extra time he was working. Other than two officers who had taken Flora's statement on the three separate occasions, the police had done nothing to help. Frustrated, Adam had admitted that he felt better that Flora had Mitch on site and promised to go through the camera footage with her again when he could.

In the meantime, though, Mitch had worked wonders in the gardens and Flora knew Billy would be smiling down on his efforts. It was all coming together so nicely for the great Choux Competition that weekend. In a supportive nod to Harry's condition, Sally had gently suggested to Betty that the event could be postponed, but Betty would hear no discussion of such a thing. She was determined that, although she herself wouldn't attend – for the first time in some thirty odd years – as she would be sitting with Harry like she did most days, the other ladies shouldn't miss out.

"Just you show that Witherham bunch who are the best bakers!" Betty said, her fighting spirit showing through the frail shadow of her former self that she had become in recent weeks.

"I'm sure we will," Sally had reassured her, all whilst quirking a worried eyebrow in Flora's direction.

It was later that week, when Flora was putting the finishing touches to the large front sitting room in the manor house, that she heard a loud banging on the front door. She carefully laid down the delicate hand-made tie-backs that she had been about to place around the curtains – all ordered from a little independent seamstress shop in Alnwick – and hesitated before going to answer it. The decorators had finished the day before, and the room clearance couple were coming back next week to see what Flora had decided on doing with all of the junk they had found, yet any of them would have knocked on the back door, as would Flora's friends. The noise disturbed Reggie, who was sleeping on his perch in the corner of the room.

"Get out of it!" He shrieked, following it up with, "Somebody else! Not that jerk!" for good measure, as if by throwing a good few insults at the sound it would miraculously go away.

The hammering continued, however, and Flora had to will her feet to move her in that direction. She smoothed her hands self-consciously over the old, faded gingham dress that she wore, opting more and more often for comfort over appearance nowadays. Her mouth dry, her heart hammering in her chest in synchrony with the sound that echoed around the hallway, she opened the heavy, old door slowly, making a mental note to have a spy hole put in this one, to match that at the coach house. To Flora's relief, it was a woman of about her own age who stood on the large doorstep, though the look on her face was anything but friendly. Even through the layers of make-up and bright red lipstick, Flora could see the wrinkles caused by her anger and frustration.

"Can I help you?" Flora asked, glancing at the woman's hand curled into a fist, ready to strike the door again. The sound of swooping feathers came up behind her, and a rather irritable bird landed on Flora's shoulder. She silently willed him to keep his beak shut.

"Oh, hello," the visitor didn't have the grace to look sheepish for the din she had caused, simply jutting out her chin and looking Flora up and down in undisguised perusal. She herself was wearing a form-fitting red dress which hugged every curve and squashed her ample chest up into a cleavage which resembled a ski slope – smooth, white and with a steep downhill curve. Flora felt like a lumpy giant in comparison and for a brief moment a wave of jealousy washed over her, though she knew deep down that even at her slimmest she would never have exposed quite so much flesh, even in her twenties.

Flora didn't like to think she was one to judge someone solely on appearance, but that didn't stop the rather critical thoughts which ran through her head. Then again, she supposed, the woman had been banging on her front door and was now looking at her like something the cat dragged in, so she had a right to be a bit unforgiving in her mental assessment. Reggie, however, had no such restraint, "You old trout!" he squawked, leaning his whole body forwards to

85

emphasise the point.

"Well, I never! Anyway, you must be the housekeeper," clearly the woman had finished her own assessment of Flora, and had come to that conclusion. It was the second time in the past few weeks that Flora had been mistaken for the hired help. She herself held nothing against people for what they did for a living, but it irked her that the label was being attached to her because of her appearance – that she had failed to scrub up enough to be recognised for who she was.

Reggie had sensed the newcomer's unspoken dismissal of him and, never one to be unwillingly silenced, continued his tirade, "You old goat! Stupid woman!"

"Enough!" Flora warned him, realising that the bird must have heard her call herself a stupid woman and was now repeating it. The thought made Flora sad – she really ought to be kinder to herself.

"That bird needs to be taken care of…"

Pulling herself up to her full height, her back ramrod straight in her annoyance, Flora assumed her haughtiest tone and cut the visitor off before she could continue, "Flora Miller, owner of the estate. And you are?"

A flash of shock registered on the woman's face, before she plastered on a fake smile that was almost as big as her ample chest, and held out a well-manicured hand, "Missy Christie, pleased to meet you."

Flora shook the woman's hand tentatively, her mind whirring as to what the purpose of her visit could be. She decided to forgo the pleasantries and just ask outright – living with Betty was clearly rubbing off on her, "And the reason for your visit is?"

"I'm looking for my fiancé."

TWELVE

"Fiancé?" Flora squeaked, her attempt at sounding cool and assured falling flat. Visions of Adam flew through her mind, and her first thought was to say, 'he's my fiancé,' but she held her tongue, and was glad she had.

"Yes, Mitch D'Alessio. Tall, tanned, body like a Greek god…"

Again, Flora felt the need to stop the woman from finishing her sentence. Goodness knows what she would have come out with next and, unlike a lot of the women in the village, Flora hadn't been affected by Mitch's good looks or his more-than-adequate physique. She had assumed by his surname that he had Italian heritage but, other than that, Flora hadn't pondered on him further, "Ah, my gardener, yes."

Flora felt her body slump slightly in relief that she did not personally have to deal with the woman and that it wasn't herself whom she was seeking so aggressively.

"Yes, have you seen him?" Missy's eyes flashed as she looked around her at the wide lawns and flower beds which sat in front of the manor house, as if Mitch would suddenly materialise from behind a rhododendron bush.

"He is having a day off today," Flora didn't really want to give the woman much information – not that she was privy to Mitch's whereabouts in his personal time anyway – just enough to get her to leave, "I have no idea where he is, but he's not here."

An uncomfortable silence stretched between them, and a small tic on the side of her face caused Missy's right eyelid to flutter in annoyance.

Reggie, who had given the impression of having relaxed into a silent sulk on Flora's shoulder, took that brief moment of awkward quiet to shriek, "You old trout!" and to fly into Missy's face. Her scream was as high as the red stiletto heels on which she now toppled backwards. Luckily, Flora reached out a quick hand to catch her elbow, as she called off Reggie's attack.

"Reginald Parrot! Inside now!"

Reluctantly, the bird left his perch on top of Missy's head and flew past Flora, not looking back once. The woman herself was still shrieking, one arm held by Flora, the other patting her head dramatically, though Flora suspected she was more worried about her well-coiffed hair than anything else. She needn't have worried, it clearly had on enough hairspray to withstand a tornado let alone a small – albeit naughty – parrot.

"Flora, are you okay?" the gruff, male voice came from behind her, and Flora was relieved to be able to release the woman into Mitch's care. She did feel rather sorry for him, it had to be said, seeing the look which came over Missy's face. Flora could see the moment the woman spotted the gardener behind Flora's shoulder, and if her glaring eyes and steely hard line of her mouth were anything to go by, Mitch was not going to get off lightly for whatever misdemeanour had aroused Missy Christie's wrath.

Flora released Missy's arm and tried to shuffle backwards, away from the pair. They were standing in the small porch which led to the large entrance hall, and there wasn't much room to manoeuvre. As it was, though, Missy stalked forward regardless, her eyes fixed on Mitch like a lioness who has spotted her prey, wedging Flora between them.

"I, ah, I should be getting on…" Mitch mumbled from behind her.

"Oh no you don't!" Missy said, launching herself past Flora, who ended up flattened against the cold wall, and grabbing onto Mitch's shirt with both hands, "I didn't come over from Witherham for you to ignore me! I haven't seen you properly in three weeks! Three weeks, Mitch, a woman has needs…"

The last words were said on a plaintive wail, and if Flora wasn't thoroughly uncomfortable before then she certainly was now. Thinking that the situation couldn't possibly get any worse, Flora looked to Mitch, about to tell him to move to the side and let her pass, when Phoebe came from behind him carrying two large glasses of something fizzy and saying, "Mitch, love, I thought we could have these in be…"

For a brief moment, the only sound was of Missy's ragged breathing, until suddenly all hell seemed to break loose. Reggie, who had followed Phoebe back to the scene, no doubt drawn by the noise and the tension in the air, started shrieking, "Secrets! Secrets and Lies!" whilst at the same time Missy shouted in Mitch's face, "Who on earth is she?"

Flora finally managed to squeeze past the pair, raising her eyebrows at Phoebe, who simply handed her the tray wordlessly and turned back to confront Mitch and the woman who was still clawing at his chest. Reggie had settled on Mitch's head and was clucking "You sexy beast!" as if he was happily here for the show.

Shaking her head and muttering to herself, Flora carried the tray of drinks back to the kitchen, distracted by the shouting she could hear echoing along the hallway behind her. Looking up as she entered the bright room, Flora let out a shriek of her own, the tray falling from her hands and crashing to the floor, where the glasses shattered and the bubbly liquid formed a pool around the shards. Standing in front of her, the light of the open back door shining behind him and casting him in shadow, was a behemoth of a man. They stared at each other for a second, Flora's mouth open on a second scream – silent this time – and the man's face scrunched into a frown. He reached up to brush ginger curls back from his forehead and made a strange clucking sound with his tongue, as if deciding whether it would be best to speak or to remain silent. Flora couldn't have spoken even if she'd wanted to, what with the fear lodged in her throat as it was.

Reggie, who must have flown to find Flora upon hearing her cry out, had no such qualms, and flew straight at the stranger, shrieking, "Off with ye! Stupid jerk!" in the manner of his former owner.

Seeing the strange little bird – who had landed to sit on Flora's shoulder protectively –seemed to pull the man back to the situation at hand, and he tilted his head slightly to side, speaking in a soft Scottish brogue, "Sorry to have startled ye lass, the door was open and I saw ma Phoebe slippin' in here."

"Your Phoebe?" Flora squeaked, wondering if the morning could get any more bizarre. What was this tangled web she had inadvertently become caught up in?

"Aye, I followed her up from the village, with that, that…" his face turned beetroot red, as if from the force of holding his tongue and not swearing in front of Flora, "that wee maggot she was fawning over."

"Wee maggot!" Reggie shrieked, mimicking the phrase exactly and apparently thrilled to be adding to his catalogue of inappropriate insults.

"Yes well," Flora was recovering herself now, and anger was replacing the fear, "It is rude, illegal even, to enter someone's property without permission. What if there'd been a, a guard dog?"

The man raised his auburn eyebrows high into his forehead, his eyes focusing on the little bird on Flora's shoulder, clearing trying to hide an amused smirk, "Aye, could've been scary that!"

"Hmm," Flora stared him in the eye as best she could from her lower position. The man was a giant, he must have been at least six foot seven, and broad to match. His blue eyes were kind, though, and she felt some of the tension leave her rigid shoulders, "I'm Flora Miller, and you are?"

"Lachlan McBride, apologies for not introducing myself. Seeing them together…" his hands balled into fists, "well, my manners seem to have upped and left me."

"Indeed," Flora was about to go on, to suggest he seek Phoebe out at Jean's, at a more appropriate moment, when the shouting behind her became louder and the sound of Missy's shrieking voice assaulted her ears.

"You get back here, Mitch, don't think you can brush me off! I'm not sitting around at home like a lovesick puppy waiting for you to deign to visit me and explain!" The sound of a stilettoed heel stamping on the tiled hallway floor swiftly followed the outburst.

"I already told you last week that it was over! Come

on, Phoebs, let's get out of here…" Mitch came to an abrupt stop as he came up against Flora in the kitchen doorway. He had been looking backwards, pulling Phoebe along behind him, with the wailing banshee who was Missy close on their heels, and had almost run straight into Flora.

Yet again, Flora was sandwiched between people she didn't even know. Reggie evidently felt trapped too, and took off from her shoulder, doing laps above their heads. For a brief moment, all were silent and only the whooshing sound of feathers in flight could be heard.

"Lachlan!" Phoebe's voice was a shocked whisper as she leant around Mitch and Flora to take a look at what was causing the hold up.

"Phoebe, lass, come here," it was said gently, but there was no denying the command in the man's voice.

"She's not going anywhere! Who are you, anyway?" Mitch asked, apparently not fazed by the man's size nor the thunderous expression he now wore. In what Flora considered a rather ill-thought out move – not that she supposed either man was doing much thinking – Mitch let go of Phoebe's hand, leaving her with a furious Missy whose bosom heaved from the force of trying to restrain her temper. He walked past Flora, stepping carefully over the mess on the floor, and stood chest to chest with the newcomer. Mitch was tall, at over six feet, but he seemed dwarfed by Lachlan.

"Come on outside, little boy, and I'll show you what happens when you mess with ma girlfriend," Lachlan's voiced rolled from his chest in a low rumble.

"No!" Missy shrieked, pushing Phoebe out of the way and into Flora none too delicately, "He's mine! Don't you dare touch a hair on his head, you, you ape!" She launched herself at Lachlan, hammering her fists at his chest, as he swatted her efforts away as if she were a bothersome fly.

Phoebe began sobbing and moved in front of Flora, wringing her hands helplessly, "Don't hurt him," she whispered, flashing a longing look in Lachlan's direction.

"I really don't think there's any chance of that," Flora said drily.

Mitch looked embarrassed, that a woman was fighting his battle for him Flora presumed. At length, Lachlan lifted Missy away gently and placed her over by the sink under the window behind him, turning back to Mitch with eyes bulbous from fury.

It was at that point that something snapped inside Flora. Her patience, she later concluded. Clapping her hands loudly, as one would at the front of a class of pre-schoolers, she shouted, "Enough!" startling even herself with the ferocity and volume of the single word. All eyes turned to her. Even Reggie ceased his swooping and landed quickly on the counter top. The ensuing silence was a blessed relief compared to the previous assault on her senses, and Flora breathed in slowly through her nose.

After a few deep breaths, and with all eyes still on her, Flora finally spoke again, "This is my home. I may not live up here, but I treat it with the same love and care. I enjoy peace and quiet, and this," she swept her arm around to indicate all four of them, "this is not acceptable."

"Sorry Flora," Phoebe whispered, her eyes still brimming with tears.

The men echoed her sentiments, though Missy said nothing. Flora took another deep breath, "Mitch, you and I will talk later about the boundaries I'm going to need to put in place if you are to continue lodging here. For the meantime, I'd like you all to leave."

"Flora, please, I had no idea…" Mitch began, his brown eyes round and pleading like a puppy dog's.

"Not now," Flora said, more sternly this time, "I'm due down at the tearoom. I had expected to be finished my final touches up here by now." She ushered them all out the back door, feeling quite exhausted by it all.

"Good riddance!" Reggie shrieked three times, as he watched the strange group leaving from the comfort of Flora's shoulder. Phoebe was hurrying off ahead of both men, who were jostling to catch up with her, whilst Missy was intermittently clinging onto Mitch's arm, as he kept shrugging her off. Her shoes weren't a good match for the gravel, so the woman kept stumbling and in the end simply couldn't keep up with the others, shrieking her defeat in a sort of wild howl.

Flora turned away, letting out a long sigh, and went back inside to clean up the mess on the kitchen floor, to finish her few tasks and to collect her handbag. *What was it about this place that it attracted so much negative energy?* she wondered. *Was it the things the old house had seen? With Harold, but before him even.* Flora wondered if she should ask Reverend Marshall to come and bless the place, or pray over it, or whatever might clear the lingering shadows and allow positivity and blessings to flow. She added it to her mental to-do list, enjoying the softness of Reggie nuzzling into her neck.

"Come on, old bird," she whispered, "we make a good

little team."

"My old bird," Reggie echoed, and Flora couldn't help but smile, realising she probably shouldn't have used that term. She could just imagine him calling Tanya an old bird, and the thought of her friend's likely reaction caused Flora's smile to widen.

THIRTEEN

Saturday rolled around too quickly for Flora. The good news was that Harry had come back to them! The doctors were happy with how his breathing was improving since coming off the ventilator, and Flora and Betty had both cried by his bedside to hear his voice. It felt almost miraculous – certainly, Flora felt that her prayers had been answered. Whilst Harry's illness had forced her to stand more on her own two feet, Flora had been permanently distracted for the past few weeks, worrying for the couple. Since Harry was to remain in hospital for the time being, Flora and Reggie were still staying with Betty – something which Flora was happy to do, but which was leaving her even more exhausted than usual. Between the hospital visits, and the uncomfortable nights on their spare bed, Flora was more than ready to get back to her own little home in the next few days.

"We don't have time for daydreaming," Edwina Edward's sharp voice brought Flora back from her musings. She didn't get along with the woman at the best of times, but the doctor's wife had been insufferable since she'd arrived at The Rise at eight o'clock that morning to help get everything ready for the event. This was the last in a long line of instances in which Flora had to bite her tongue to avoid giving the woman a piece of her mind.

Sensing the tension, Sally came over to join them, "It's all ready now, Edwina, we need only to have a pot of tea while we wait for the Witherham ladies to arrive."

"It was all ready before she even arrived," Flora muttered under her breath, feeling put out that her efforts of the past week had not been appreciated or credited. She was being churlish, she knew, but really she just wanted to get this pastry competition over with. Her own secret attempt at making éclairs in the kitchen at the tearoom had been a disaster, the pastries being too flat to even infuse any cream into them, so she had arrived this morning with only Betty's entry – strawberry and white chocolate profiteroles. The sight

101

of them sitting on the kitchen table in Betty's little cottage had made Flora's mouth water.

A large table had been placed in the bay window of the sitting room at the manor house, and covered in a hand-embroidered tablecloth courtesy of Jean who was now rearranging the plates of entries from the Baker's Rise ladies for the umpteenth time. Even Amy had managed to produce a delicious-looking batch of mini banana custard éclairs. The other half of the table lay empty, waiting for their competitors' hopeful creations and poor Reggie had been shooed into the study, lest he contaminate any of the treats on display.

"It looks grand, Jean," Sally reassured her, directing the older woman to one of the new velvet sofas which had arrived the week before. Flora was very happy with her choices for this room, the pastel tones and classical designs giving a calming effect.

"No one can beat your elderflower and meringue eclairs, Jean," Tanya declared, waltzing into the room with a large pot of tea and a plate of biscuits on a tray, "you're onto a winner there!"

On hearing this, Edwina gave a disapproving 'tsk' and sat on the wingback chair in the farthest corner of the room, no doubt put out that her fruit-filled choux buns with caramel sauce had not received more of an accolade. She couldn't have set herself more apart from the other ladies if she'd tried.

"I don't know about that," Jean said humbly, "but Phoebe did wolf two down yesterday evening, so I guess they got her seal of approval at least. Now, where is that girl? She'd better not be making moon eyes at the gardener again, they've given me nothing but worry since she arrived! She's meant to be taking over from Peter in the shop in ten minutes."

Jean made to rise, but Flora interrupted her, "I'll go and look for her, Jean, you stay put."

Flora didn't know whether Jean knew of Lachlan's visit, and she certainly hadn't wanted to be the one to tell her, so she thought to have a quiet word with Phoebe and check that everything had been sorted. Mitch had been avoiding Flora since the showdown the other day, or so she thought by the fact her gardener quickly disappeared behind a bush, or up the stairs every time she came within view, and Flora had been grateful. She had no desire to get involved in the soap opera that was his life.

"Flora!" Phoebe exclaimed as Flora entered the sunlit kitchen. The young woman's face was red and her expression guilty before she quickly turned her face back to the counter. The back door clicked shut, as if someone had just left, but Flora barely registered this, feeling too uncomfortable about the conversation she was about to have.

"Phoebe, we're having tea in the sitting room so perhaps you could join us? Though on second thoughts, your aunt did mention you're expected back at the shop?"

"Ah yes, I was just, ah…" Phoebe moved to the side as Flora came up behind her, "just putting this éclair on a plate for Mitch. It's one of my aunt's and I thought no-one would notice one missing." True enough, a pretty china plate sat underneath a paper napkin on which the word 'Mitch' had been handwritten followed by a love heart. Atop the napkin sat a delicious-looking éclair.

"Oh, that's very kind, Phoebe, if I were you I would put it on his shelf in the fridge – the one he's labelled – to keep it fresh and make sure he gets it," Flora smiled at the young woman's efforts, then steeled herself to ask, "so, I'm guessing you and Mitch are…"

"Still together," Phoebe blushed.

"Okay, and the man from Scotland?"

"Gone back? Who knows? Why would I care?" Phoebe

shrugged her shoulders in what Flora thought of as a rather childish manner, considering the man had felt enough for her to chase her down the country, and proceeded to place the plate lovingly in the fridge.

"I see, well the Witherham ladies will be arriving any time now," Flora added, it having suddenly dawned on her that Missy Christie's name was on the list of entrants and the last thing Flora wanted right now was to referee a standoff between the two women. She needed this event to go smoothly, so that her life could hopefully return to a level of normality in the next week.

"Yes, I'll be off," Phoebe said, flashing Flora a smile that belied none of the awkwardness that had just passed between them, "see you later Flora!"

"See you later," Flora replied distractedly, her mind already back on the competition ahead.

FOURTEEN

The sound of barking and yapping drew all of their attention to the front window some ten minutes later, where sure enough a gaggle of ladies could be seen exiting a rather fancy, luxury minibus. The noise came from a gang of dogs which Flora immediately recognised.

"She couldn't have… she hasn't brought the dogs, has she?" Flora asked Shona, astounded.

"Oh yes, she takes them everywhere, never leaves her little 'dahlings' at home," Shona replied, doing a perfect impression of Lavinia Errington's cut-glass accent as they followed the other women to the front door.

Everyone moved aside to let Flora through – even Edwina, though she clearly did so rather unwillingly – as lady of the manor she should be the one to welcome their rivals. Feeling better dressed than the last time she had met the Lady of the Withers, Flora smoothed down her beautiful peach tea dress and opened the door wide, plastering a smile on her face.

"Dahlings! Behind me!" Lavinia Errington ordered, and the little terriers, each with a diamante bow in their fur, followed her in a winding train once again as she advanced on the front door. Flora heard Shona snort behind her and tried hard to stifle her own giggle as they filed past. What Reggie would make of them, Flora could only imagine, and her stomach did a little flip at the thought.

The other ladies from Witherham followed behind the excitable canines, and then a well-dressed man who looked to be a butler of some sort trailed along last, pushing a trolley – *they brought a tea trolley, really?* – which Flora assumed held all of their choux-based entries for the competition. Each woman was welcomed by Flora with a hand shake and a smile, until Missy Christie appeared before her. Flora held out her hand, but the other woman simply brushed past rudely, refusing to make eye contact.

"Charming!" Tanya exclaimed, having witnessed the exchange – or rather, lack of it – from her position next to Flora, then added in a stage whisper, "And what is she wearing?"

Flora looked at Missy's retreating form, her leather mini skirt barely covering the essentials, and thought for a brief moment about Tanya's own, rather similar, taste in clothes. She said nothing though, agreeing that Missy looked rather… what was it? Overdressed? Underdressed? Flora wasn't sure which, but it certainly wasn't the usual 'uniform' of the W.I. members, that's for sure! Even Tanya had chosen a knee-length navy dress in honour of the annual occasion. It had multicoloured dinosaurs on it, of course, but Flora appreciated her effort nonetheless!

When everyone was assembled in the front sitting room, and the prized pastries had been suitably displayed, Flora stood to welcome everyone to The Rise and to the annual competition. Rather awkwardly, Lavinia Errington stood at the same time, obviously used to being in charge, her dogs taking up almost half of one of Flora's new sofas – much to Flora's chagrin.

Embarrassed and unsure, Flora said nothing, simply stood wringing her hands. Lady Errington had no such nerves or uncertainty and opened her mouth to begin, just as Tanya spoke up, "Thank you, Mrs. Miller, for having us all."

This was the prompt which Flora needed, and she spoke quickly then, ignoring Lavinia's look of displeasure. The formalities dealt with, Amy and Shona offered to go through to the kitchen to make the hot drinks, whilst Flora judged the entries. Missy sidled up beside her, peering out of the window as if looking for someone. Flora presumed the woman was searching for Mitch and so said nothing. She certainly didn't want to stir that hornet's nest again.

"If you squeeze any closer to the window, you'll squash the pastries," Lavinia spoke harshly, coming up behind Missy and causing the other woman to jump in surprise. There was clearly no love lost between the two, Flora surmised, as Lavinia continued, "You'd better not be looking for my nephew!"

"No, of course not," Missy shuffled back, the blush rising from her chest, exposed by her low-cut top, up to her face.

The only man out there was the chauffeur-come-butler who had accompanied the Witherham women, so Flora assumed Missy had already set her sights on someone else, her gardener quickly forgotten. Flora wondered briefly why the Errington's would hire their nephew as staff and even make him wear a silly uniform, but it was really none of her business and nothing about that couple would surprise her, so she turned her attention back to the task at hand.

Flora hadn't anticipated that she would have to eat, at least a partial amount, of each of the twenty or so choux creations on offer, and she gave a sad thought to her hips before beginning on the first, a lemon and passion fruit profiterole wreath, created by none other than Lady Errington herself. That is, if one didn't believe the rumours that she hired someone to do the job for her! If she was jealous of her counterpart's supposed efforts, Flora didn't let it show, simply setting one of the plump profiteroles free with a small dessert knife and placing it on her delicate floral plate.

She had barely lifted the treat to her lips, however, when there was a huge commotion from the study next door.

Jean and Tanya were quick to accompany Flora to investigate the noise, only to find that the team of terriers had managed to push open the study door and find Reggie, who was not happy at being disturbed from his nap.

"Tina the Terror!" he shrieked, repeatedly divebombing their little heads, not caring that Tina herself wasn't in fact in the group. The dogs went berserk, yapping and snapping at the parrot, and Flora had to shout for Lavinia to come and call them off.

Lavinia tutted and fussed at being drawn from the main room, rebuking Reggie for disturbing her dahlings.

"Well, I think it was rather the other way around," Flora said, indignant, as Reggie snuggled into the crook of her neck, taking shelter.

The two women stood staring at each other for a moment, with Tanya muttering to Jean about little menaces, and flashing angry eyes at the canine intruders. It was then that Amy popped her head into the room, "Ah, Flora, would you have a minute to come to the kitchen?"

Flora's heart sank at the thought of another problem as, judging by the expression on Amy's face, whatever she had to show her wasn't good.

"I'll take these babies out to Spears. He's waiting with the transportation, and can take them for a walk," Lavinia Errington said, her tone harsh, as if nothing would put her out more than dealing with her own animals.

111

Reggie followed Flora into the kitchen, where she was immediately assailed by a horrible smell. It was eggy and gassy and so strong, that Flora had to put her sleeve over her nose to try to filter it out of her senses. Shona had opened the back door wide, and was stood in the doorway gasping in lungfuls of air. Reggie was also making a strange choking noise and had hid his head under his wing.

"Reggie, go and find Jean," Flora ordered, shrugging him from her shoulder in the direction of the hallway and sending him to sensory safety, "What on earth is that smell?"

"Is it the drains?" Shona asked, her eyes red and streaming, as her words were cut off by a cough.

"I don't know, but I think I'm going to be…" Amy rushed past Shona, and outside where she promptly threw up. Flora felt so sorry for her pregnant friend, that she had been exposed to… to whatever this was. She herself followed outside to look for Mitch, who she knew was working in the grounds somewhere today, though Flora herself had suggested that he keep away from the main house for the duration of Missy's visit.

Flora went around the back of the house, in the direction of the ornamental garden looking for her gardener, when she was surprised to see another, altogether different, male figure up ahead of her. Her heart began to race, and her temper to rise.

FIFTEEN

"Lord Errington!" Flora snapped at the man who was about to disappear around the far corner of the gardens ahead of her. He was walking fast, obviously keen to leave the vicinity of the house, and barely slowed even though he must have heard Flora's call.

"Errington!" Flora shouted again, louder this time, and she ran to catch up with him, despite her sore ankle protesting the sudden movement.

Her breaths coming short and fast, her face red, Flora eventually caught up with the man, who at least had the good grace to stop when he heard Flora's heels clicking quickly on the path behind him.

"Mrs. Miller," Errington smiled easily, as if there was

absolutely nothing wrong or unexpected about him being found here.

His attitude added fuel to Flora's internal fire, and she stood with her hands on her hips as she caught her breath. Errington looked her up and down with an infuriating expression of pity, until Flora bit out, "What are you doing here?"

"Oh, I was just waiting for my wife," the words rolled off his tongue easily enough, but Flora saw the man's eyes shift to the left avoiding her piercing gaze. She didn't believe him for a second.

"You didn't arrive with the ladies," it was a statement and not a question, and Flora saw the line of Errington's mouth harden.

"I followed on foot. It's a lovely day for a walk."

"Indeed. A very long walk, at that. It must be at least six miles through the fields. And you didn't happen to smell anything odd as you arrived?"

"Smell?"

He was so smooth, so slick and slimy Flora thought, though she knew she didn't have the time to have it out with the man now, making unfounded allegations would be pointless, "Yes, follow me back to the house.

You might be able to help. Then you can have a drink and wait for your wife." Flora said the last part with more than a hint of sarcasm in her voice as she walked back the way she had come, listening to make sure the man was following her.

"Tanya, have you seen Mitch?" Flora asked, as her friend met her at the side of the manor house next to the kitchen. She was stroking Amy's back while Shona held a glass of water out to her.

"Yes, he was talking to Lady Errington out the front. I saw them through the sitting room window before I came to find you all. Should I fetch him?"

"Yes please, thank you Tanya. Now, Lord Errington, can you smell that?" Outside the back of the building the smell was even worse.

"It smells like something has died," Errington replied, smirking.

Flora wanted nothing more than to wipe the smile from his face, but instead looked up at Mitch who was running towards her.

"Flora, what can... eugh! What's that smell?"

"Exactly, Mitch, exactly," Flora snapped, "Please could you investigate."

"I'll help him," Errington offered, exchanging a glance with the gardener.

"Very well, we'll close all the doors between the kitchen and the sitting room and hopefully the front of the house won't be too affected," Flora let out a slow sigh and followed the other women back into the house. The event was ruined. She knew that. All she could do now was to judge the choux as quickly as possible and get the visitors on their way.

Barely a sound could be heard as Flora approached the sitting room, being sure to close the kitchen and hallway doors behind her, and checking that Reggie was safe back in the study again. Flora opened the window in that room wide so that he could get some fresh air in there, before hurrying to join her guests.

Flora felt the strange atmosphere as soon as she entered the room, where all of the women – both Baker's Rise and Witherham – were gathered in a circle around the chair in the far corner. Undrunk cups of tea and plates of half-eaten pastries dotted the room, as if forgotten in haste.

"Is everything okay?" Flora asked, a feeling of dread creeping up her spine. She was getting a good instinct for trouble now, and her gut feeling was so strong in this moment that Flora felt she herself might be sick.

"It's Lady Errington," Tanya turned to face Flora, a worried look on her face, "she's feeling, ah, rather out of sorts."

The ladies parted to let Flora through, until she was standing face to face with the woman who sat shaking, her face a ghastly white and her skin clammy like unrisen dough.

"Lavinia?" Flora asked gently, kneeling down in front of her, "What happened?"

Gasping for breath, Lavinia stuttered, "I don't know, I feel... stomach hurts like..." the poor woman didn't manage to finish her sentence before she grasped her throat, bent over almost double and then threw up over Flora's front. The group of women jumped into action then, some helping Lavinia to her feet and towards the bathroom, others moving to get Flora cleaned up.

This involved Flora going to the main bathroom upstairs, and she was just hurrying back down when she heard Edwina Edwards on the phone in the main hall, requesting an emergency ambulance.

"Flora," Jean came rushing from the direction of the downstairs cloakroom, the usually unruffled woman breathing heavily and speaking too quickly, "Flora, come quick, it's Lavinia, she's passed out and we can't get her to come around again."

"I saw Errington out back," Flora remembered suddenly, "could you get him, Jean? He'll want to be with his wife, I'm sure."

"Of course, of course," Jean held her hand to her chest as she rushed off in the opposite direction.

"I'm a nurse, retired, but still," one of the Witherham women who was kneeling beside Lavinia said to Flora as she entered the tiny space, "It's serious. She needs medical help as soon as possible. I've checked her airways, her pulse is very weak. She seemed to have some sort of convulsion before she stopped, stone still."

Lavinia was laid out on the floor in the recovery position, a cool cloth over her forehead, and Flora sank to her knees alongside.

"Lavinia! Love Bunny!" Errington's strong voice could be heard coming up the corridor, and he soon appeared in the doorway ahead of Jean, "Oh my Lord! What happened?"

Flora stood to let the man have her space, where he kneeled over his wife, kissing her cheeks and whispering words of love. Flora turned away, feeling she was intruding on a private moment. What she wouldn't have done to have Adam with her right now. As it was, Flora found herself silently praying for the woman on her bathroom floor, who was clearly seriously unwell. Several of the other women were praying out loud in the hallway, led by the vicar's wife, and Flora could hear their whispered words and muffled sobs. It was a long way from the nearest ambulance depot to their tiny village, and she was acutely aware they might be in need of a miracle right now.

SIXTEEN

It had been a long day. Long and so, so sad. The paramedics had been unable to revive Lavinia, and she had passed away in the ambulance on the way to the hospital, her husband by her side. Flora had barely known the woman, and was far from being on friendly terms with the couple, yet she felt the passing acutely. Lavinia Errington had become unwell in Flora's home, the cause of her illness as yet unknown, and Flora felt responsible. The sudden onset and strange symptoms were red flags which would definitely need to be investigated, especially since the Errington's had friends in high places, on whom Rupert Errington had immediately called. And so it was that Flora had already had a lengthy visit from the dour detectives

Blackett and McArthur, with whom she had become rather too well acquainted since moving to the village. They had interviewed every woman present at the manor house, not allowing anyone to leave until this task was complete, and taken all the baked goods and samples of the teas and coffees away for testing. Apparently, with the speed at which Lavinia had become ill and subsequently died, poison was the most likely suspect if her passing was found to not be from natural causes. Flora was holding onto hope that it had been a cardiac arrest – still tragic, but not quite as awful as the alternative, another murder in the village.

As she watched McArthur gathering up the evidence with a uniformed officer, Flora couldn't help but notice the napkin that sat on the empty plate next to the wingback chair where Lavinia had taken unwell. The name Mitch was clearly visible under the half-eaten pastry, and so too the little heart which Flora herself had watched Phoebe draw earlier that day. This observation had soon been forgotten, however, in the chaos of the hours which followed. The Witherham ladies had been understandably very upset, and it had been dark outside before the police had let them leave. Flora had been worried for Amy, who looked ill and exhausted. Despite everyone's suggestions that she lie down upstairs, her friend had insisted on soldiering on until they had all eventually been allowed to leave and a grim-faced Gareth had arrived to take her home.

Finally, Flora found herself alone with her feathered friend. Reggie had been perched on the study window sill when Flora had come into the room, and she was surprised that he hadn't gone outside for a fly around. *Something must've kept him entertained*, Flora thought. The smell from the kitchen permeated through the whole of the downstairs now, though thankfully it became fainter the farther you went from the kitchen.

"I've phoned a drain clearance company, they work seven days a week, so can come out tomorrow morning. I'll make sure I'm around," Mitch said, joining Flora in the study, "Would you like me to walk you home?"

"Thank you, Mitch, but Adam is coming to collect me, any time now," Flora said absentmindedly, "thanks for organising that, by the way."

"Not a problem, happy I can help," Mitch's face was sombre and Flora could tell he had been affected by the day's events, "the two detectives are coming back to interview me tomorrow, so I'll be here anyway."

"That should work!" Reggie chimed in, "A good job done! Out in no time!" Flora hadn't heard him say those phrases before, but her brain was too foggy now to dwell on it. At the rate the little bird was picking things up, he would be speaking in whole paragraphs soon!

"Are you sure you're alright love?" Adam's face peered at her through the gloom inside the car. He had switched the engine off and they were parked up outside Betty's cottage.

"Yes. No. I don't know. Sorry, you've driven all this way to see me and I can't seem to think straight long enough to have a conversation."

"Don't apologise," he took hold of her hand gently, holding it between both of his and stroking Flora's palm with his thumb, "You're probably in shock. I feel awful that I've been so absent lately. They've drawn so much manpower onto this case I'm on, and we're all working all the hours we can. Not that that's a good enough excuse. I feel like I've neglected you."

"Tsk," Flora shook her head, "I'm not a child who needs looking after, Adam. Of course I want to spend all the time I can with you, but I understand the nature of your job. It's an important thing that you do. Besides, it'll be easier to see each other when I'm back in my own cottage." She leant over the middle console and rested her head on his shoulder, feeling her eyelids droop.

Flora's stomach rumbled loudly between them, "Please tell me you've eaten today?" Adam's forehead scrunched into a frown.

"I, ah, well with everything going on, no, I forgot," Flora turned away to try to hide her embarrassment – after all she had just told him she could look after herself and her body had contradicted her straight away.

"Oh love, I should have brought some takeaway. It's late now, and when Betty gets home from the hospital she won't feel like cooking either."

As if summoned by his words, headlights appeared at the bottom of Front Street and a car ambled along the road at a snail's pace, eventually coming to a standstill in front of them. The vicar was at the wheel, with Betty sitting next to him, clutching her handbag on her lap. The vicar nodded to Flora as he helped Betty out of the car and to her front door. The man himself looked exhausted, and Flora knew that Sally would have told him about Lavinia Errington's death. *Perhaps he could do with a break*, Flora wondered, then caught herself. She couldn't keep worrying like this about every other person she met, it was enough that she cared for herself and Betty tonight, as well as the small, green-feathered chap who was squawking from his carrier on the back seat.

"Will you come in?" Flora asked Adam softly.

"I , ah," she could see the battle unfolding across his features – he wanted to stay but needed to go.

"I understand," Flora interrupted before her fiancé could say anything else. She reached up to peck him on the cheek and then left the car silently, reaching into the back seat to grab her unhappy bird.

"Be careful up at the big house. Call Pat Hughes if you've any concerns at all," Adam's voice carried after her.

"Come on Reggie, you deserve a big fruit salad," Flora whispered, holding the little case up to her face. *Bird diets be damned!*

"No!" Betty exclaimed when Flora had given her a brief account of the day's events. With being at the hospital all day, for once the rumour mill hadn't reached her yet, something she seemed quite put out about, "And you didn't even pick a winner?"

"Ah no," Flora replied, thinking that was the least of it, but not saying so, "this year will have to be declared void."

"Excellent," Betty muttered, before catching herself, "I mean, ah, that I'll be able to take part next year... poor woman, of course."

"Of course," Flora was too tired to think. Too tired to eat. She had fed Reggie, although she'd noticed earlier that he had stuffed himself with all the seeds in the bowl on his perch in the study. This would be his second dinner, but she didn't care. The little chap was guzzling down the apple slices and segments of orange as if he hadn't been fed for a week, and the sight of him so contented made Flora happy. Well, happier at least.

"I'll make us a pot of the good stuff, lass," Betty said, tapping Flora on the arm, "and some toasted sandwiches."

"You don't have to do that, Betty," Flora yawned, "I should be looking after you."

"And you have been. For the past three weeks! The doctors said today that Harry can come home in a few days, if he has regular home visits from Dr. Edwards, so you can get back to your little house tomorrow if you like?" Betty rubbed Flora's shoulder in a maternal caress, "But for now, you sit there and tell me again about the different choux buns and éclairs…"

At least it took Flora's mind off the grislier events of the day. She had to admit that the thought of being back in her cosy coach house was very welcome!

Very welcome indeed!

SEVENTEEN

Flora and Betty both missed church the next day, as Flora drove Betty to the hospital and then returned to her friends' cottage to pack up her things. She had been back to the coach house regularly, of course, to collect clothes and return others, to sneak a quiet hour out of a busy day, but the thought of returning properly now brought a quiet euphoria that Flora hadn't felt in a long time. The sun was shining down, the trees in the village were in full blossom, and Flora could almost forget the hideous reality that another murder investigation was taking place up at the manor house.

She and Reggie had just arrived back home, and the kettle was just beginning to boil, when Flora's mobile phone rang. Hoping it was Adam, so that she could say all of the things she wished she'd said the previous evening, Flora was simultaneously disappointed and concerned to see that it was Mitch.

"Flora?"

"Hi Mitch, is everything okay? Did they get the drains sorted?"

"Yes, some kind of ammonium sulphide mixture – a 'stink bomb' for want of a better term – had been poured in, they think. It must've been in a large amount to cause that smell for that long."

"So it couldn't have been a natural blockage?"

"Unlikely," Mitch breathed in sharply, drawing the word out and Flora got the distinct impression that wasn't the worst of what he had to say, "probably foul play."

"Well, it was definitely foul. Does it smell any better now?"

"Yes, it's all disappeared, I've had the windows in every room open all morning. Flora, ah there are a lot of police here, milling around," the man's discomfort was clear in the way his usually suave tone was now stilted, "and they're asking to see the security footage. I said we didn't have any cameras. We don't, do we?"

"Actually we do, yes, I'll be right up, tell them to wait," the last thing Flora wanted was to tell Mitch about the secret room off the study which housed the recording hub. It was her closely-guarded secret and, for reasons even Flora wasn't sure she could fathom, she intended to keep it that way.

"I can go through the tapes with them," Mitch began to offer, but Flora cut him off quickly.

"Five minutes, Mitch, see you soon."

It took Flora a moment to compose herself when she reached the manor house, the sight of the forensics team clad in their white overalls, and the uniformed officer standing guard at the back door brought memories flooding back – ones she would rather forget. Mitch was waiting in the kitchen for her, his mouth set into a grim line.

"I'd hoped to keep you from all this," he spoke softly to Flora, indicating the house with a sweep of his hand, "they've mainly been focusing on the front sitting room, and the small cloakroom where the lady took bad."

"Don't worry, Mitch, it's my responsibility as the

owner of the estate to be here. Thank you, though," she added, appreciating his care, "Have they been through your room yet?"

"My room? Why would they want to? I mean she didn't go in there, and I'm not sure I've even mentioned that I live here," he spoke fast, a small sheen of sweat appearing on the man's forehead.

"Well, I have… some experience with these things, I'm sorry to say, and even if the police haven't outright asked you, believe me it's still better to volunteer the information so that they get the full picture as early in the investigation as possible. When you've done that, why don't you head off now that I'm here? Go to visit Phoebe, maybe?"

"Phoebe? No, we're not together."

"Really? She seemed to think you were a couple yesterday," Flora hoped that her gardener wasn't playing fast and easy with the young woman's heart, "did you not see the plate she left you in the fridge?"

"I've been trying to let her down gently since that brute of a boyfriend arrived. Plate?"

Flora was about to reply, when Detective Blackett appeared from the hallway, "Ah, there you are Mrs.

Miller," he snapped the words impatiently, as if she was already in trouble, like a child who had skipped class.

"Yes, I'm right here. Good afternoon, detective."

Blackett grunted, as if struggling to see the good in anything, his face tilted to the side so the angle made his beaky nose look like a thin pencil, "We expected you here first thing this morning, we certainly did not expect that you would leave the hired help in charge."

Flora noticed Mitch bristle beside her and sought to intervene, "Mitch, thank you for your help today, I'll see you tomorrow. Detective Blackett, you should therefore have been more precise in your stipulations yesterday."

The young man looked to Blackett, who had scrunched his eyes up in disdain so that only thin slits remained, opened his mouth to speak, then thought better of it, tipped his cap to Flora and left. Flora let out the breath she had been unconsciously holding and directed her full attention to Blackett, keeping her back straight and her shoulders back.

"Very well, detective, let's look at this security footage, then any of the rooms you would like me to show you."

Seemingly surprised by her easy acquiescence and cooperation, one of Blackett's eyebrows raised higher than the other, though he said nothing other than making a strange clucking noise with his tongue. The sound reminded Flora of Reggie, whom she'd left cosy in the coach house, and she wasn't sure whether she wanted to giggle or cry.

It was a long, headache-inducing afternoon. They had studied the CCTV footage in the secret room, propping the door open as Flora still hadn't worked out how to release it from the inside, and going through all the videos from the previous morning twice. Blackett planned to take the footage away with him as evidence, though Flora wasn't sure what good it would do for the investigation. The cameras were situated down the side of the house near the kitchen door, to the front – but only angled towards the large wooden front door – and to the back as far as the rose garden. They didn't cover the whole expanse of the back of the building, as there were no doors there, just a set of stone steps that led down to the basement, the hatch for which was locked from the inside. Certainly, there were plenty of drains where a liquid could have been added without being recorded – not that Blackett was interested in the petty vandalism, but Flora thought she might as well look for clues while the detective kept his beady eyes on the bigger picture.

There was of course footage of the Witherham ladies arriving, and Flora thought she might have heard a laugh from Blackett for the first time since she had made his unfortunate acquaintance. It sounded more like a snort, and was quickly muffled behind his hand, but the man's lips had twitched into a small smile when he saw the first couple of dogs jump from the minibus. By the time all eight were out, and toddling along in a little line, the small noise erupted from the man's mouth, despite his obvious attempts to quell his reaction. Flora caught Blackett's eye, and then the two of them were chuckling. It was a strange moment of shared humour, and one which significantly reduced the tension in the room. The mirthful expression relaxed Blackett's features, so that Flora saw a completely different man for the briefest of moments. He was not jovial by any means, and the curtain of stoicism and detachment soon dropped back into place as if it had never been lifted, but Flora knew what she had seen and for the first time she could understand what Adam referred to when he said his colleague was actually quite a ladies' man. Up until now, Flora had thought maybe Adam was speaking ironically or joking with her, but these few moments had let her see

135

the potential truth in it.

Not that it mattered. It was a brief moment of brevity in an otherwise serious time, and Flora's mind had a way of flitting to happier, easier thoughts. It was as if there was only so much talk of death that she could take.

"That's interesting," Blackett muttered, rewinding the tape for a third time. Flora couldn't see exactly what he referred to, having left her glasses back home, just that he was focused on the large bushes at the front of the house.

"What is it," she whispered.

"There," he pointed a long, thin finger at two blotches above the top of the farthest rhododendron in the picture, "That I believe is your gardener's cap, and that, next to him, I believe is the head of the deceased."

Flora gasped, "Lady Errington? With Mitch? How strange. I mean, I knew he had done some work up at The Withers, but she wasn't one to speak freely to the staff as far as I'm aware."

"Quite so," Blackett replied, his lips pursed in concentration though he refrained from sharing his views further. He made notes in his pad, jotting down the exact time that the pair were seen.

Flora's head ached. There was more going on here than met the eye, of that she was certain, she just couldn't quite put her finger on what it was.

EIGHTEEN

McArthur arrived just as they were finishing up with the security footage, and Flora offered both detectives a cup of tea. It was as she bent down to get the milk out of the fridge, that she remembered the plate that Phoebe had left in there for Mitch the previous morning, the one that had somehow ended up beside Lavinia Errington.

"A napkin with his name on it, you say?" McArthur asked between mouthfuls of fruit scone, clotted cream and jam. They were sitting at the rather foreboding dark wood dining table, in Flora's most-disliked room in the house, as the forensics team were still working in the sitting room.

"Yes, I watched her put the éclair in the fridge for

Mitch to have later, all labelled up and then spotted the plate again when you were here collecting the food to analyse. Has anything come back about that?"

"It's too soon," Blackett jumped in, never one to want to share information with members of the public, "we don't even know the lady died under suspicious circumstances yet. Ordinarily, none of this would even be started until we have the results of the post-mortem early next week, but with Lord Errington being a golfing buddy of the Detective Chief Superintendent..." Blackett let the sentence hang, his meaning clear. Flora understood, of course, that certain people received preferential treatment. It had always been that way, so there's no reason why it would have changed. She hoped that people didn't start treating her differently, if she ever did move into the manor house herself.

"So, can you just go through the sequence of events one more time, please Flora?" McArthur expertly changed the subject, "Including where everyone was at key points in the morning, if you can remember."

Flora let out a small sigh, but then did as she was asked, this time remembering to include how she had seen Rupert Errington outside as well.

"Really? That's interesting," Blackett took out his

notepad and added the information, as McArthur had been the one noting down until that point.

"Yes, he's been after buying the property, actually," Flora expanded, describing all of her interactions with Errington to date, and highlighting the spate of petty crimes which had been targeted at the house as well, "I wonder if someone is trying to force me out, make the old place too much of a hassle to keep."

The fact that Flora implied Errington might be involved in such a scheme was not lost on Blackett, who seemed to already harbour a strong dislike of the man along with the power he carelessly wielded, "I think you may be right, Mrs. Miller, it would certainly seem that way."

"Could those incidents be connected to the death?" Flora asked tentatively.

Blackett became a closed book again, "Only time and a police investigation will tell." He emphasised the word 'police,' no doubt lest Flora and her friends begin their own snooping. Flora had no intention whatsoever of doing such a thing, simply wanting the searches in her house to be completed as quickly as possible.

"So, just to clarify," McArthur took up the questions again, reading from the notes she had taken, "the gardener lodges here, in a room upstairs, and you do not know where he was living before that, though you believe he has done some work over at The Withers. The young lady who left him the choux pastry lives with her great aunt above the grocer's store here in Baker's Rise, though she is only visiting, and it was this same aunt who actually baked the éclair. The lady, ah Phoebe, yes, Phoebe is in a rather new relationship with the gardener, though he insists it was a passing fling which is now ended, due to her former boyfriend having threatened him the other day – the man having arrived unexpectedly from Scotland. One of the Witherham women also lays claim to the gardener's affections, and was part of last week's altercation." She took a deep breath in, and looked to Flora to confirm the details.

"Exactly," Flora agreed, glad she wouldn't have to try to explain the whole thing again, "oh, you don't think Mitch could have been the real target, do you? I mean, if there was in fact an intended target. Do you think the victim was really meant to be Lady Errington?" The thought had just occurred to Flora, but now it seemed startlingly obvious.

Blackett and McArthur exchanged a pointed look, and Flora knew not to push further.

"If we could just see the gardener's room, Flora?" McArthur asked, giving a longing look at the remainder of her scone which sat uneaten on the pretty china plate, "I think you've already shown us the rooms the deceased visited."

"Of course," Flora led the way up the first flight of stairs, the sweeping staircase bathed in light from the high hallway windows.

When they reached the small room which Mitch used as a bedroom, at the far end of the landing, however, Flora was as equally surprised as the two detectives to find both a padlock and a key lock on the door.

"Is this really necessary?" Blackett barked.

"I shouldn't have thought so, though he is very private, and we have been subject to these minor attacks, so to speak," Flora found herself waffling. They couldn't access the space without Mitch, so the two women went back downstairs, Blackett huffing behind them.

Flora's ankle was aching, and her mind whirring with a myriad of possibilities as she saw the detectives and their team out. They had promised to be in touch as soon as they had the lab results, though Flora wasn't sure she wanted to know the truth of it. Ignorance was surely bliss, and she'd heard enough bad news since she moved to Baker's Rise to last her for a very long time to come.

NINETEEN

Monday dawned bright and warm, with the promise of a sun-filled day in their small corner of Northumberland. Flora and Reggie were at the tearoom early, and Flora had baked two batches of fruit scones by the time Tanya arrived for her shift. She was working in the tearoom every day now, while Flora was dividing her time between the tearoom, bookshop and manor house. As well as visiting Harry and helping Betty, Flora had felt herself spread quite thinly between her different ventures. She was glad that the coming week seemed likely to follow a relatively normal schedule, for the first time in a long while – on paper at least. With the exception of taking Betty to collect Harry, on whatever day the doctors said he could be discharged later in the week, Flora was hoping for a quiet life.

Any hopes of forgetting the potential murder investigation which loomed over The Rise were swiftly dashed, however, with Tanya's keen enquiries as to what she'd missed up at the big house the previous day. Her husband, the local policeman, had not been involved in any investigation yet – given no-one knew the cause of death – so she hadn't been able to pump him for information as she usually would! Flora explained the detectives' visit in as few words as possible, and deliberately omitted the part of the discussion which focused on her gardener's colourful love life, and her own suspicions regarding the murder target – if indeed there had been one at all.

Tanya listened in rapt interest until they were interrupted by the tinkling of the little bell above the door. The tall figure of a man blocked out the light from the doorway for a moment as he entered, the breadth of him filling the whole space, and Tanya let out an audible gasp. Flora would have felt amused at the way a blush rose up her friend's cheeks and her eyes were out on sticks, had she not recognised the visitor immediately.

"Mr. McBride, good morning! I hadn't expected to see

you still in the village," Flora realised some of Betty's bluntness was rubbing off on her, in the way she often came straight to the point now.

"Good mornin' Mrs. Miller, lovely little place you have here," Lachlan stooped to fit under a low, wooden beam which hung just inside the door, and smiled easily at the two women.

"Please, take a seat," Tanya squeaked, gesturing at all the empty tables. Flora had noted in the past that her friend was always one to be affected by a good-looking man, and this time was no different.

"Thank ye," Lachlan lowered himself onto the chair nearest Reggie's perch – not a wise choice, Flora thought, though she said nothing.

Sure enough, the little bird sensed the movement and the change in the air, and pulled his head quickly from where it had been nestled under his wing as he snoozed.

"The fool has arrived!" he shrieked, flapping his wings in agitation.

"Reginald Parrot! Shush!" Flora reprimanded him quickly, as she saw Lachlan's bushy eyebrows raising in shock at the outburst, "My apologies, Lachlan."

"Not at all, he's a feisty wee chap, eh?"

"He certainly is," Flora agreed ruefully, "now, what can we get you?" Tanya had already furnished the man with a menu and a brilliant smile.

"Actually, I was after a bit of advice," the big man seemed unsure now, running his hands over his wide beard and gesturing to offer Flora the seat next to him.

"Would you mind getting us a pot of tea, Tanya please?" Flora asked, as she sat down, her mind running a mile a minute as she wondered what he might want help with. She sincerely hoped it wasn't anything to do with Phoebe or their relationship.

"Thank you," Lachlan paused as if gathering his thoughts, and stared up at the little bird who was eying him warily from his perch above. Flora was shocked, therefore, when the large Scot raised his hand and Reggie jumped straight on to it, allowing himself to be brought up to the stranger's face.

"Get out of it!" Reggie clucked, but he made no move to fly away, simply nuzzled into the man's beard. Flora had seen photos up at the manor house of the late Harold Baker, in which he sported a rather straggly, unkempt beard and she wondered if the visitor reminded Reggie of his former owner.

"Oh you're a wee softie at heart, aren't ye?" Lachlan whispered and Reggie bobbed his head up and down and lifted one foot then the other in a happy little dance.

"I think you've made a friend for life," Flora smiled, as a large piece of chocolate cake appeared in front of Lachlan – as much to his surprise as Flora's – and then a pot of tea appeared. When Tanya took a seat next to them, Flora thought to tactfully give her another task to complete, perhaps in the bookshop, before quickly thinking better of it and hoping that her friend might make the coming conversation slightly less uncomfortable.

"So," Flora began, when the tea was poured, and the Scot had taken the biggest bite of cake she'd ever seen!

"Aye, thank you, Flora, it's just that I can't seem to bring myself to leave your funny little village. Not without Phoebe by my side, or knowing she's going to follow me home soon, at least."

"That must be very difficult," Flora replied, in a deliberately none-committal tone.

"Aye, it is that, I mean we've had our ups and downs, but she upped and left without telling me, and now I realise what a big bampot I've been all along. How much she means to me, ye ken?" His Scottish brogue became stronger the more emotional the man became.

"Maybe she just needed a breather?" Tanya said, kindly, "Normally if a woman leaves abruptly, she has a good reason." Flora knew that Tanya had her own painful experience of this, and nodded gently at her friend.

"Aye, I understand that, I do, but I cannae stand the thought of her with that eejit gardener."

"I'm not sure how we can help…" Flora began.

"Sorry, aye, let me get to the point. I went round to that wee shop yesterday, and there she were, crying behind the counter on her auntie's shoulder. Fair made my heart burst outta ma chest seein' her like that. She's normally so bonnie, and her eyes were swollen with tears, I just wanted to hold her," he whispered, as if knowing he was over-sharing, "They would nae tell me what the upset was about, just that it was to do with a death up at your big house. So, I thought I'd see what you could tell me, Mrs. Miller?"

"Oh," Flora was wringing her hands on her lap now, visions of a napkin with a love heart, a woman lying prostrate on the floor, and two surly detectives filling her mind, "Well, a lady from a nearby village sadly passed away and we have all been shaken by it." As for whether Phoebe might have more of a reason to be upset, Flora certainly didn't want to speculate.

"Aye, I came up that day, just to look fer Phoebe yer understand, and saw the minibus and all the activi…" Lachlan clamped his mouth shut halfway through his sentence, and shuffled uncomfortably in his chair. Reggie, who was snuggling against the man's broad chest now, sensed the new tension in the air and flew back to his perch silently.

"You did?" Flora asked as nonchalantly as possible.

"Aye, but only for a quick minute, before Auntie Jean saw me out the kitchen window and told me Phoebe was back down in the shop. She didn't even give me her normal lecture, seemed she wanted me outta there fast like."

"What was she busy with in the kitchen, if you don't mind me asking?" Flora's throat felt dry and the question came out quite husky.

"Somethin' to do with a cream bun on a pretty plate, I think, but I didn't see it for more than a couple of seconds, the look on her face was enough to send me scrabbling!" Lachlan gave a low laugh, no doubt at the thought of a big man like him being scared off by one look from Jean, but Flora didn't share in his humour. In fact, a feeling as heavy as lead had settled in her stomach.

"Well, it was very hectic up there that day," Tanya replied so Flora didn't have to, "I would suggest you go back to Scotland and give Phoebe the space she needs." Any harmless flirting Tanya may have been inclined to participate in when the man had arrived, had swiftly been replaced by a sisterly solidarity with their new friend. Phoebe may only be a temporary visitor to the village, but the women already saw her as one of their own and treated her as such.

"Aye, yer probably right," Lachlan swallowed his cup of tea in one go, reached up to tickle Reggie's chin, and stood, causing the whole table to rattle as he tried to accommodate his legs, "how much do I owe you?"

"Oh, on the house," Flora said absentmindedly, the sadness of knowing she would have to mention this conversation to the detectives the next time she saw them, already washing over her.

Neither of the women saw the visitor out, simply saying a quick goodbye and then clearing the table as if on auto-pilot. Tanya didn't even know about the éclair that had been separated from the others and left in the fridge, and yet she seemed as unsettled as Flora.

"Strange goings on again," Tanya whispered as they both placed the china crockery onto a tray.

"Strange indeed," Flora replied miserably.

TWENTY

The rest of the day thankfully passed without incident. There was a steady stream of customers in the bookshop, enough to keep Flora busy in there, whilst Tanya manned the tea room. When the door tinkled just after half past three in the afternoon, Flora was delighted to see Sally Marshall enter with all three girls in tow.

"Ladies!" Flora greeted them, making little Charlotte giggle.

"We're not ladies, we're girls," she whispered shyly, peeking out from behind her mum's leg.

"I know, but you're so well behaved I keep forgetting your real ages," Flora winked, earning her another giggle from the older two.

"Come on Reggie, you can be the dragon!" Evie exclaimed, holding out her arm and watching as the little parrot landed smoothly.

"How are you doing?" Sally asked quietly, once the girls were happily playing princesses and dragons in the book shop, and the three women were ensconced in the tearoom, enjoying some banana bread and a pot of Earl Grey.

"We had a visit from Phoebe's Scottish boyfriend this morning," Tanya launched into a detailed description of the man, and Flora pretended to listen though her mind was elsewhere. She assumed Sally had actually been referring to the weekend's events, and that was where Flora's thoughts were too.

"Well, that sounds rather complicated," Sally said politely, when she eventually got a word in edgewise, "and how about the… incident up at the big house?" She looked sideways as she spoke to make sure there were no little people within earshot.

"I'm still waiting to hear back from the detectives," Flora said, her voice low, "though I fear it doesn't look good. They didn't seem to hold out much hope that Lavinia died from natural causes."

"So awful," Sally replied, "my James went up to The Withers yesterday after church to see Rupert Errington, and told me afterwards that the poor man is in bits. That he doesn't know what to do with himself, and those little dogs are running riot and creating havoc up there. James thinks he could do with some peace. Errington had said that his nephew had visited, though, which is nice and was apparently of some comfort."

"Oh?" Flora's ears perked up, "I thought the nephew worked there as the butler or chauffeur or something? Wasn't he the one who drove the ladies across on Saturday? Why would he need to make a special visit?"

"I'm not sure about that," Sally said, "James didn't mention his name, and didn't bump into any relatives while he was there... such a tragedy."

"It really is," Tanya replied, while Flora kept silent as her mind whirred loudly inside her head.

"Guess what, Miss Flora!" Evie said, skipping in from the bookshop to take a bite of the muffins Tanya had brought to the table for the girls, and interrupting the adults' conversation.

"What would that be?" Flora smiled, pulled from her

internal musings.

The girl hopped onto Flora's lap, her face red from excitement, "My daddy says he's spoken to the Big Boss up there," she pointed heavenward, "and that we can have an animal service after all! So Reggie can come to church!" The girl let out a squeal, which drew the attention of her sisters and had them also racing through to join the group. Sally caught Flora's eye and raised one eyebrow, as if she thought the whole idea slightly preposterous, though she smiled indulgently at her daughters.

Flora couldn't imagine what a church full of animals would sound – or smell – like, but she smiled widely and exclaimed, "Well, Reggie will have to be on his best behaviour for that!"

"Ha! Not likely!" Tanya added, shaking her head as Reggie swept through and landed on the woman's head, exclaiming "she's a corker!" and making them all giggle.

Flora had planned to head up the driveway to The Rise after closing up the tearoom that evening, but she somehow couldn't bring herself to make the short journey. For whatever reason – partly she thought, because of recent happenings, both the death and the spate of worrying attacks, but also because deep down Flora couldn't face a one-to-one conversation with Mitch right now – she turned the other way and walked quickly with her feathered companion back to the coach house.

The inside of the cottage felt warm and welcoming, the old stone walls having been heated by the sun throughout the day. After kicking her shoes off, Flora phoned Betty straight away to get an update on Harry and then, satisfied that he was still heading in the right direction medically and that Betty was cosy at home for the night, she went through to the bathroom to run a deep bubble bath.

Bath, food, television, and maybe a cheeky glass of red, Flora thought contentedly, as she filled Reggie's bowl up with sunflower seeds and then retreated to her bedroom to choose a pair of comfy pyjamas. No sooner had she turned off the water, and unclipped her hair from the bun that had held it up all day, however, the front doorbell rang. Thankful that she wasn't yet undressed, Flora sent a prayer heavenward that whoever it was could be easily dismissed.

Reggie cocked his head towards the sound from his spot on the kitchen table, but even he couldn't be bothered to see who was visiting them this time. So Flora hurried down the narrow hallway alone, remembering at the last minute to look through the spyhole in the door before opening it.

"Adam! I didn't expect to see you tonight," Flora exclaimed, walking into his arms for a hug before the man had even entered the house.

"Sorry, I should have called first. It was a… a kind of impromptu visit actually."

"Don't apologise, you know you're welcome anytime," the happiness in Flora's voice was unmistakable, and she tilted her head to get a better look at her fiancé, "Oh Adam, you look a bit peaky. Is everything okay? You haven't come down with that stomach bug that's doing the rounds?"

"No, no nothing like that," Adam followed Flora into the house, still in his smart suit she noticed.

"You came straight from work," it was more a statement than a question, and Flora felt her heart beat faster as she began to think that maybe his call wasn't purely social.

"I did, love, I did. I'm not on duty tonight, I probably should've gone home for some much needed kip, but, ah…" he trailed off, instead kissing Flora sweetly on the cheek.

She wasn't distracted by his affection this time however, "Something specific brought you here. And not just my beautiful face and witty conversation," the joke fell dead as Flora saw that Adam's mouth was turned down into a frown.

"Exactly. I wish it wasn't the case, and of course I jump at any chance to see you, especially in this busy season we're both in, but, ah…" he didn't seem to be able to simply spit it out, which was unlike the man she loved.

"There is news about Lavinia Errington," Flora finished the sentence for him, her gut telling her that this was the case.

"Yes," Adam let out a long sigh, "and it's the worst kind, I'm afraid."

TWENTY-ONE

When they were both comfortable on the settee in her little sitting room, Flora with a glass of wine, and Adam with a strong coffee, neither having wanted any food to accompany them, Adam began.

"So, I was just about to leave the office, when Blackett took a call from the coroner's office. The post-mortem had literally just been completed and he had the results on the cause of death, so I hung around till Blackett came off the phone," Adam scrubbed his chin with his hand, and Flora could see the five o'clock shadow which he was sprouting. It was quite thick and long, making her wonder if her fiancé had even managed to get home the night before. The fact that he was here, instead of going back to his place to rest, both touched her and worried her at the same time.

"So you came all this way to tell me in person," Flora whispered, taking one of Adam's hands in hers.

"I did, I wanted to be here when you got the news, wanted to be the one to tell you and to give you a big cuddle," Adam squeezed her hand, "You'll have to feign ignorance when Blackett tells you tomorrow though, love, as you know I'm not meant to share this information. It isn't even my case…"

"I know, I know, and I'm so grateful," Flora leant in and kissed him softly on the cheek until Adam turned his face slightly so that he could capture her mouth with his. It was sweet and tender, and a brief respite from the hectic times and enforced absences they had endured recently.

Pulling away with a reluctant sigh, Adam whispered, "Any more of that and I'll forget why I'm here," he cleared his throat, the sound rough and continued, "the post mortem found evidence of poison in the deceased's liver, kidneys and heart, more specifically Aconitum poisoning."

"I've never heard of that," Flora spoke through her fingers, as her spare hand was now covering her mouth in shock.

"It's common name is Monkshood or Wolfsbane. It's actually a pretty plant, which can grow wildly, but it is exceptionally poisonous – both to the touch, absorbed through the skin, but especially in the tubers and roots. If someone ground up even a small amount of these roots, then they could add them to anything and make it poisonous. In olden days it was used as a poison for arrowheads when hunting wolves, hence its name. It's so fast acting, the poor animals would have given up without a struggle."

"Would someone not know it was there? That they were swallowing it, I mean?"

"It does taste foul and bitter, but if it were added to something sweet…"

"Like a choux pastry," Flora's lower lip trembled.

"Exactly. Aw love, try not to get upset, we can't change anything now. I just wanted to give you a heads up," Adam stroked Flora's hair gently.

"Oh, and what if there was already a foul smell in the air, that we could all almost taste…" Flora's mind was whirring again.

"Well, yes, that would mask it even more."

"Oh my goodness!" Flora tried to speak more past the

lump in her throat, but it was useless. She had to let the tears fall. Adam's arms were instantly around her, pulling Flora into his chest and holding her tight.

"It's okay, love, I've got you. Let it go."

Reggie, who had been happily half-dozing on his perch, watching the couple with one eye open, now came fully alert and swooped over to land on Flora's shoulder.

"Good bird, good bird," Adam whispered, lifting the hand closest to Reggie from Flora's shoulder and stroking the parrot's soft back.

"I'm okay," Flora found the strength to sit upright again, "I expected it, it's just still a shock…"

"Of course," Adam replied, "that's why I wanted to be here and tell you myself."

"What about the lab tests on the food and the crockery?" Flora had a sinking suspicion she knew what his answer would be.

"One came back positive, as far as I could tell from Blackett's conversation – a napkin with a name on it?" Adam wasn't sure what that referred to, but Flora knew straight away.

"The napkin that was under the éclair Phoebe left for Mitch," she whispered, "poor girl, will she be under suspicion now?"

"I would think so, love, and anyone else who could have got hold of it."

"Well, anyone could. It was chaos there for a while, what with the dogs and Reggie, the horrific smell, people going into the kitchen to make drinks and such, and unexpected arrivals. Oh, what a mess!" Flora felt the tears begin to fall anew and tried to scrub them away. They made her feel weak, and she knew she was going to have to be strong in the coming days.

Adam gently moved her hands and used his own thumbs to wipe away her tears, making Flora feel cared for and cherished, "Listen, love, you don't need to have any part in this, other than letting the detectives into the big house, and answering their questions. They will interview everyone, they will connect the dots and find the missing pieces of the puzzle. And when everything is out in the open, when this case and my own investigation are complete, let's set a definite date for the wedding. It's killing me being apart so much."

Flora accepted his kiss eagerly, and then whispered, "Me too, I want nothing more than for us to be married."

They snuggled down on the sofa for a moment, with Adam's arms cradling her, and Flora resting her head on his chest. Her errant brain continued to process the new information, though, and suddenly Flora sat up and said, "I had a thought earlier, that Lady Errington may not have been the target at all. If the éclair was meant for Mitch, then surely he was the intended victim?"

"Possibly, love, possibly, but no one can tell at this stage. Let the detectives do some digging, eh?"

Flora nodded and snuggled back down, though her anxious mind wouldn't rest. She stroked Reggie's feathers as he sat on her knee and enjoyed the warmth of Adam's embrace, but inside she felt the chill of knowledge.

The knowledge that another murderer was on the loose in Baker's Rise.

TWENTY-TWO

After Adam had left, and Flora had taken her bath, she had sat for a long while in the kitchen with a cup of chamomile tea. Her body was exhausted and aching, but her mind wouldn't rest, her heart often racing and her hands clammy as if in a state of panic. Even when she'd dragged herself off to bed, she had tossed and turned, unsettling Reggie who had chirped, "My Flora! My Flora!" over and over from the pillow next to her.

Thus Flora woke early, feeling as if she'd had no rest at all, and surprised by the ping of a text message coming through when it was barely even seven o'clock in the morning. She had taken to keeping her mobile phone by her bedside, ever since the frightening incident with Martin Loughbrough, so that she could always call for help if needed. Flora had never felt this unsafe, even living in London, and it saddened her that in this beautiful, peaceful part of the country she would know anxiety like never before. Doctor Edwards had told her that she probably had a mild case of post-traumatic stress disorder following the attempted strangulation, and Flora agreed with him. Not that giving it a label helped her at all. Perhaps when they were married and Adam moved in, her fears would subside – so Flora hoped, anyways. She had also missed being able to talk things through with Harry, never wanting to burden him with estate business on her visits to the hospital. He would have had some wise words about the petty crimes up at the house, and about Mitch, she was sure.

The message was from Lily up at the farm, saying that they had her godson and his little family come to give them a hand for a few months, but as he was actually a botany graduate he was hoping to get some experience doing some landscape gardening and identifying the flowers which grew wild in the area. She wondered if there would be an opportunity for him up at The Rise, maybe shadowing Flora's new gardener. Flora replied to the text, saying that she would of course be able to offer him something of that nature over the coming weeks, and would they be able to meet her up at The Rise later that day. Flora thought to introduce the young man to Mitch and then leave them to it to make the arrangements. She had too much on her plate right now to get involved in anything else.

With that agreed, Flora had just dressed and was making some porridge for breakfast, when her phone made another noise – this time an incoming call, "It's busier than King's Cross in here today," she moaned at Reggie, before answering.

"Mrs. Miller?" The clipped tones of Blackett were immediately recognisable on the other end of the line.

"Detective Blackett, to what do I owe the pleasure at this early hour?" Though Flora was pretty sure she knew why he had called.

"Yes, my apologies for the timing, the early bird catches the worm and all," it was the first time Flora had ever heard the man apologise, she wondered if their shared moment of humour in the secret office had softened him slightly towards her, "I was hoping you'd be up and about, and free to meet McArthur and I up at The Rise first thing?"

"Yes, of course," Flora wanted to get the conversation over and done with as quickly as possible, so that she could get on with her day and let the detectives get on with theirs. The sooner they began their interviews with the villagers, with Errington and with Missy

Christie, the sooner the investigation would hopefully be concluded.

"Perfect, shall we say half an hour? We are already en route to Baker's Rise."

"See you then," Flora went to pour boiling water from the kettle into her cafetiere-for-one and noticed that her hand was shaking as she slopped the water over the sides.

"Silly bird," Reggie commented, rather unhelpfully, from the corner of the table where he was guzzling grapes. Flora didn't have the heart to restrict his diet, she was simply planning on avoiding him meeting with the vet until things had settled down and a stricter meal plan was on the cards.

"Hmm," Flora replied, wiping up the spill with a dishcloth, "perhaps you should stay here while I go up to the big house. I'll take you to the tearoom later."

As if he had understood, Reggie flicked a piece of grape skin in Flora's direction and shuffled his feet so that his long tail feathers were now angled towards her. Flora felt well and truly dismissed!

Whilst the early morning sun shone down on Flora as

she walked up to the big house, there was a distinct chill in the air and she pulled her cardigan closer around her. Blackett's car was already visible, parked on the gravel driveway outside the manor as Flora rounded the top of the hill, and she took a deep breath, steeling herself for the conversation to come.

"Shall we go inside?" Flora offered, leading the two detectives down the side of the house and unlocking the back door which was always her preferred entrance to the house. The key for the heavy, wooden front door was too big and cumbersome to carry around, at least that's what Flora regularly told herself. In reality, she simply still felt like an interloper who should sneak in, rather than the owner of the property who had every right to be here.

They entered the kitchen, to be met with the sight of Mitch bending over to look in the fridge in only a pair of boxer shorts. Unaffected, Flora coughed loudly to announce their presence, while she noted a distinct red blush creep up McArthur's neck.

"Good morning, Mr. D'Alessio," Blackett had no need for subtlety and Flora watched as the startled young man turned to face them, "it is fortuitous that you are up and about so early, as we were hoping to have a conversation with you, as soon as we've spoken to

Mrs. Miller here."

"Oh yes, well I'm actually out in the grounds all day. Out on the petrol mower," Mitch spoke quickly though showed no embarrassment of his under-clad state, "Perhaps this evening? Oh, have you any news on how that poor woman died?" He asked nonchalantly, as if speaking about whether the weather would be good for cutting the grass.

Blackett's face tightened in displeasure and Flora was glad that she wasn't the one on the other end of his steely glare, "In that case, we will speak with Miss McIntosh and her aunt in the shop before coming to seek you out, but it will be at our convenience and not yours!" He made no reference to the question regarding the cause of death.

Mitch barely batted an eyelid at the mention of his erstwhile girlfriend, simply shrugged his shoulders and carried the whole jug of milk from the room, sauntering into the hallway as if he owned the place. The sight irked Flora somewhat, but she had more important matters at hand.

"Would you like a hot drink?" Flora offered, at the same time realising that anything they requested would have to be drunk black as her gardener had just taken all the milk upstairs.

"No, thank you," McArthur appeared to have recovered herself, her cheeks having gone back to their normal colour, "perhaps just a quick sit down in the dining room?"

"Of course," Flora led the way, noticing Mitch's gardening overalls laid out over the radiator in the hall. He was certainly making himself at home. Flora was glad that she had her little coach house to retreat to and didn't have to share the space with him. Not that that would be at all appropriate anyway, she mused.

Brought back to the present by Blackett graciously pulling out a dining chair for her, Flora sat primly, with her hands clasped in her lap.

"I'm afraid it's not good news," the detective began once he had taken his own seat opposite, "the worst, in fact."

Flora listened as Blackett and McArthur took turns explaining the findings of the post mortem and lab tests. She nodded sombrely, but said nothing, not wanting to give away that she already knew the information they were imparting.

"That's… simply shocking," Flora finally spoke when their explanations were finished, "the poor woman."

"Indeed," Blackett's face was grave, "so we will need access to this house for a while longer, as we continue our investigations in earnest."

"Of course, of course," Flora agreed, "though you don't need me to be present up here all the time, do you?" The thought sent a shiver down her spine.

"No," McArthur smiled kindly, "you can give us a key for the back door if you like, then we can come and go as needs be. Would it be okay to also invite some people over from Witherham to be interviewed here? Use this as a base, so to speak?"

"By all means," Flora reached beneath her for her handbag and produced her own key to give them. She already had copies of all of the keys for the estate on Harry's master keyring which he had made sure she knew where to find when he was taken ill.

"Thank you, Mrs. Miller," Blackett said, standing, and Flora took that as her cue to leave. Her legs felt stiff and heavy as she let herself out of the kitchen door and walked back down to collect Reggie from the coach house.

This was going to be a long, long day, and it had barely even begun.

TWENTY-THREE

Flora had told Tanya that she was dusting the bookshop. In truth, she had rushed in here the moment Janet, the post lady, had delivered the day's mail. Flora had been eagerly awaiting one book in particular, and had hoped for it to arrive in time for the choux competition in fact, but sadly it was not to be. Never mind, the beauty was here now, and Flora was sure it would help her in her quest to become a better baker. 'Fake It Till You Bake It,' the title promised, with the blurb explaining that the recipes included short cuts, quick-step-bakes, and how to incorporate shop-bought pastry into your baking so well that even pro bakers wouldn't notice. So engrossed was she in thumbing through the many photographs, and so happy for the distraction from local events, that Flora didn't hear her visitor approach and it was only Reggie's shriek of "You old trout!" that drew her attention.

I really need to get a little bell between the tearoom and bookshop, Flora thought, as she plastered a smile on her face and was given a sharp look of disapproval in return.

"Edwina, how can I help you?" Flora tried to hide the book on her legs with her arms, but it left her in a rather ungainly position, perched as she was on the tiny stool beside the counter.

"Well, I don't have time to be leisurely perusing recipes, that's for certain," Edwina said pointedly, causing Flora's hackles to rise instantly. The doctor's wife always managed to rub her up the wrong way.

The woman barely knows me! She has no idea what's going on in my life! Flora thought, but it was Reggie who spoke up for her, "Get out of it!" he shrieked, coming to land on Flora's shoulder.

"Really, have you not had that bird dealt with yet?" Edwina's look of disgust was the final straw, and Flora stood abruptly, the book falling to the floor, where she kicked it under the desk with her foot.

"Was there anything in particular you wanted,

Edwina, other than to insult me and my bird?" Flora asked sharply.

"Actually, there was, I don't have time to wander around the village socialising," Edwina rushed on when she spotted Flora's thunderous expression, "I wanted to find out about what's happening up at the big house. I saw the police driving through the village early this morning. Is there news about poor Lavinia's death?"

Flora had no idea why this woman thought she had the right to know what was happening on estate property, and said so. Following it up with, "You'll have to wait to find out like everyone else in the two villages. I'm sure it'll make the parish newsletter. Or else, ask the detectives directly, and risk standing out as a possible suspect!"

"Well, I see none of that city brashness has been polished away," Edwina exclaimed through gritted teeth, "has it not even crossed your mind that the local Woman's Institutes will be tarred by this event? I've already been on the phone to the central office to try to smooth things over."

"That was your priority? Keeping up appearances?" Flora simply couldn't believe the insensitivity of the woman, "Well, you'll be wanting to visit each lady member individually as quickly as possible, to reassure them. You wouldn't want anyone defecting to another group, would you? I hear the Warkworth and Amble W.I. has had a big influx of newcomers recently."

"Really? They wouldn't! Do you think?" Edwina had already turned to leave, muttering to herself, and Flora knew her point had hit target.

"Good riddance!" Reggie screeched as he flew to the door to watch Edwina leave.

"Reggie, don't be rude!" Flora scolded, but there was no force behind her words.

Apparently there was nowhere to find a few minutes' peace at the moment.

After a cheddar and pickle sandwich, that Tanya had insisted she eat, Flora walked back up to the manor house with Reggie flying ahead, the sun glinting off his yellow head and making it appear he had a halo. The thought amused Flora, until she was overtaken on the driveway by a rather showy Bentley. Flora didn't need two guesses to know who the driver would be.

"Mrs. Miller," Errington greeted Flora as she came up alongside the car just as he was getting out, all of the usual gusto understandably gone from his demeanour.

"Lord Errington, I am so very sorry for your loss," Flora meant the words, and looked away after only making brief eye contact, the man's acute suffering too painful to witness.

"Such a great loss," he shook his head, as if dazed that this was his reality, "detectives called me round."

As she watched the man walk toward the main door, his back hunched, Flora walked slowly around the side of the house. *Surely it would have been kinder for the police to visit the widower in his own home*, Flora mused, *unless they had some ulterior motive for wanting to see his reactions here, in the place where his wife had taken ill*.

She had just put the kettle on, when Lily's red, cheery face appeared around the back door, "Flora, it's just me and Laurie here!"

"Come in, Lily, come in. I'm just making us a cuppa and then I can show you both some of the ornamental gardens. I don't think Mitch has got around to starting on them yet, so I'm sure he'll be grateful for some help."

"She's a corker!" Reggie welcomed Lily, who was one of his favourites, then left the room, presumably to find his perch in the study.

A tall, gangly man followed Lily into the manor house kitchen. Flora figured him to be in his mid-twenties, though the floppy brown hair which half-covered his eyes and the deep tan he sported made him look younger. He had an open, friendly smile, which Flora appreciated, as she asked him what he would like to drink.

"Just a glass of water would be lovely, Mrs. Miller, thank you, I'm fair parched."

"Of course, please call me Flora," she went to get a tall glass from the cupboard next to the pantry.

"We took the opportunity of nice weather and the farm shop being closed for the afternoon to walk the back way, across the fields," Lily explained, only just now catching her breath again, "this is Lawrence – Laurie to us, as we've known him since he was a baby! He's my best friend's son, my godson."

"Very pleased to meet you Lawrence," Flora handed him the glass of water, "I hear you've studied botany at university?"

"Yes, at the University of Nottingham. Been graduated a couple of years now, just got back from taking a gap year travelling round Asia with my wife and son."

"Sounds lovely, you'll have to tell me more about your travels sometime," Flora filled the teapot with water from the kettle and made a mental note to get a new kitchen table for this room. It was awkward having to hover by the counter.

"Oh! Before I forget," Laurie began, having downed his glass of water in three large gulps, "I was pointing out some of the wild flowers in the hedgerows to Aunt Lily here, and spotted some Wolfsbane growing in a hawthorn bush, just at the back of your property. I doubt anyone goes back there much, but you might want to have it removed. Ghastly stuff."

Flora couldn't speak for a moment past the shock, so Lily added, "I wouldn't worry, Flora, it's in your farthest field, the one that backs onto Errington's land."

"I, ah, thank you, I must just, ah, give me a second…" Flora deposited her teacup quickly on the side and rushed from the room, looking for the two detectives. She found them in the dining room, interviewing Rupert Errington.

"Ah, could I have a word, Detective McArthur," Flora whispered as she knocked and then pushed open the door.

"We are in the middle of something," Blackett barked back.

"It's rather urgent," Flora spoke more clearly now, poking her head around to see the group of three who sat around the table.

"Very well, you deal with her," Blackett indicated to McArthur, who gave him a look and then came out to join Flora in the hallway.

Flora imparted the news she had just been given, and suggested the detective organise a team to go and find the plant, being careful what with it being poisonous even through the briefest contact with a person's skin.

"Should I ask Mitch to accompany them?" Flora asked, her voice low.

"No, no thank you, the fewer people aware the better at this stage, I think. We haven't made the cause of death public knowledge yet," McArthur replied, before returning to the dining room.

Flora hurried back to the kitchen, which was now empty, and then through the back door to see Lily and Laurie sitting on Billy's bench, facing the rose garden.

"Ah Mitch, perfect timing, there's someone I'd like you to meet, someone I'm hoping you can take under your wing a few times a week," Flora called to her gardener who had just come round from the front of the building, and indicated the young man who had his back to them.

Hearing her, Lily and Laurie stood to face them, as the smile disappeared from the man's face and his tone became hard, "Michael, I didn't know you worked here."

"Michael?" Flora looked to Mitch and then back to Lawrence, "You know each other?"

"Ah, in the past," Mitch muttered.

"From university," Lawrence spoke at the same time, "We were on the same course."

"You studied botany?" Flora was facing Mitch fully now, the surprise evident in her voice, "Why did you not mention it in your application?"

"I, ah," Mitch looked to Flora and then to the visitors, "It must have slipped my mind."

Flora's expression was incredulous as her mind began whirring again.

"I take it you two were not good chums?" Lily asked, attempting to break the awkward silence.

"You could say that," Laurie mumbled, "thank you for the offer, Flora, but I don't think this will work out." He turned away and left Lily looking after him in surprise.

Flora left Mitch standing where he was and walked up to her friend, who whispered, "He's always such an amenable lad, would do anything for anyone, I've never seen him react like this. Sorry, Flora."

"Not at all," Flora replied, giving Lily a hug and watching as she hurried to catch up with her godson.

When she turned to discuss the matter with Mitch, he had disappeared.

TWENTY-FOUR

Annoyed that her gardener hadn't deigned to hang
around to explain himself, Flora went to check that
Reggie was happy in the study, and to open the
window for him to get a breeze in there. She decided to
wait for the man to make an appearance, as he would
have to at some point, so that she could challenge him
on the rather obvious omission in his job application.
She felt embarrassed and angry that he had shown her
up in front of her friend, though really the error of not
checking into Mitch's background before she hired him
was Flora's own. She had taken what he told her on
face value alone.

In the meantime, Flora donned her apron and her

own, thick gardening gloves and decided to work on the replacement flower boxes out front, which she'd told Mitch – or Michael, whatever his real name was – to leave for her to do. She popped her phone into the pocket of her apron and went in search of the plants she'd had delivered from a local garden centre.

No sooner had Flora begun her task, than she felt a sharp tap on her shoulder.

"Missy!" Flora jumped at the unexpected touch and practically shouted the woman's name in her face.

"Mrs. Miller, don't you have a gardener to do these jobs for you? If my Mitch is staying over here, you should at least make use of him. Otherwise send him back to Witherham, where he belongs."

Flora was thinking that she might just do that, but didn't voice the opinion, "I enjoy arranging the flowering plants, thank you, Missy. As for your, ah, Mitch, he seems to have done a disappearing act."

"My fiancé," she emphasised the word rather too strongly, "has probably gone looking for me, to reassure me." The woman's blind faith was admirable, Flora supposed. And questionable.

Flora watched as Missy ran her hands down her figure-hugging dress in a sultry manner, and turned away before an idea suddenly came to her, "Ah, Missy, have you ever heard Mitch go by the name Michael?"

Missy cackled, the sound uncomfortable to Flora's ears, and said, "Only his aunt and uncle call him that. It's his 'Sunday' name so to speak, and he hates it."

Flora was about to enquire further, as to whether these relations lived in the area – though she supposed they must since Missy had obviously heard them speaking to Mitch – when she saw the petite figure of Phoebe making her way up the driveway. Not wanting to referee another showdown between the two women, Flora gave her hurried thanks to Missy and directed her to where the detectives had set up in the dining room, assuming that was the reason for the woman's visit.

"Phoebe, have you been summoned too?" Flora wondered why on earth the police would want to speak to both women at once.

"By whom?"

"Oh, the detectives, they haven't called you?"

"Why would they call me? I mean, I was there when the lady took ill, just like we all were, but I've nothing to say that everyone else won't also know. The other, older members of the Women's Institute will be better witnesses than me. I'm just visiting, after all," Phoebe had a look of defiance, and Flora had no intention of getting into a debate about it. Clearly, the young woman had no idea that her plated éclair was likely the murder weapon as such, and Flora had no intention of divulging that information – that was the detectives' job to do and Flora was glad of it.

Instead, Flora simply said, "Indeed," and let the ambiguity of the word hang in the air. The two women stood looking at each other for a moment, until at length Phoebe said, "I was looking for Mitch, is he around?"

"He seems to be very popular today," Flora could almost feel the wrinkles in her forehead deepening as her face turned into a frown yet again, "but no, I have no idea where he is. If you find him, please tell him that I'm looking for him."

"Will do."

"Oh and Phoebe?"

"Yes?"

"Has Lachlan gone back up to Scotland yet?"

"Why would I care where he is?" Phoebe huffed and stalked away.

Flora felt the young woman might care very much when she saw Mitch's true colours – as Flora was beginning to – she may well want Lachlan's support, not that she deserved it, and maybe even to head back north with him.

Flora shook her head gently to try to clear herself mentally of the thoughts which were crowding in too fast to process. One thing she couldn't ignore, was that Mitch seemed to play fast and loose with the truth – not just to his lady friends but also with her. Flora didn't like the idea of having someone under her roof who hadn't been completely honest with her. Seeing the new flower boxes, which Mitch had only recently hung after the originals had been torn off the front window ledges during the spate of vandalism, set Flora to thinking about the timing of recent events. It struck her in that moment that yes, Mitch had been great at helping her handle the petty crimes and clearing up afterwards, but then, hadn't these incidents only begun once he started living here?

Flora wasn't sure what all of this meant, if anything, or if her tired brain was simply trying to make connections which weren't really there so that the whole investigation could be over sooner rather than later. She sighed deeply, and decided to leave the planting for another day, tucking her gardening gloves into the wide front pocket of her apron. She would go up to see Lily and Laurie at some point soon, and would perhaps ask him to do all of the planters around the place, as an apology of sorts that his visit today had been wasted. Of course, if Flora happened to find out what had caused the man's rift with Mitch while she was there, then all the better…

Flora's legs took her automatically to the study, to the little bird who she knew could calm her racing heart and mind. Sure enough, she found Reggie perched on the window sill, in front of the open window.

"Good bird," Flora said, coming over to stroke his downy soft feathers.

"My Flora! My Flora will break soon!" Reggie chirped as he snuggled into her palm.

"What?" Flora took a step back in her shock, "What did you say, Reggie?"

The little bird cocked his head as if unsure as to whether Flora was displeased with him or not. Since she had deliberately kept the tone of her voice light and soft, he must've decided that his owner was happy with him after all, and so continued, showing off his new vocabulary, "Flora will break soon! Last lap!"

"Last lap of what, Reggie? Where did you hear this?"

Facing the open window, Flora suddenly became acutely aware of where Reggie had heard these new phrases. It dawned on her that he may have heard more, too.

"Reggie, good bird, good bird. What's new with you?"

"New? New?" the bird repeated a few times, and Flora was just beginning to get exasperated and think the whole thing pointless, when he said, "wife died, your aunt. No stomach for it now."

It was several phrases joined together, yet it made perfect sense to Flora's ears. Reggie must have heard the lines spoken several times during the conversation for him to be able to remember them so well, even with his growing talents in that area.

Flora took out her phone from her apron pocket to record him, but of course the bird would not repeat the phrases she needed him to, simply chattering on happily, running through his usual repertoire of stock sayings.

It must've been Errington speaking just outside, Flora thought quickly, *he's the only one who has lost his wife, so he must be Mitch's uncle and Lavinia his aunt. It can only have been Mitch he was talking to. Why did Mitch hide that from me? From everyone? So Errington wanted to break me, to make me sell by making the place more trouble than it's worth, but Mitch... he must've been the one doing it all. He got himself inside here, so he could have free rein to... The two-faced... and what about Lavinia?* Flora realised she was talking to herself, in an attempt to unravel it all, and the little bird on her hand was studying her intently.

"What about Lavinia?" he repeated, as the burden of this new truth weighed heavy in Flora's stomach.

What about Lavinia? Now that was the important question.

TWENTY-FIVE

Flora stood as still as a statue by the open study window, unable to decide which way to move. Should she go straight through to tell the detectives what she had found out? Or should she look for Mitch and try to establish the truth. Knowing how cocky he was, Flora doubted the man would ever admit to anything. *No,* she thought, *I need actual proof.*

Walking slowly through to the kitchen, Flora thought of Mitch's bedroom, locked up so securely. She ruled that out almost immediately, as she would never manage to break in there without being heard. That left the new shed which she'd bought him. It was padlocked, except when he was getting his tools out or putting them away. The bones of a plan formed in

Flora's mind, one which bore only a minimal risk to herself. She would wait until she saw him opening the shed through the kitchen window, then rush out and send him away on a ruse, maybe by saying that Missy was coming that way and he should make himself scarce.

Yes, thought Flora, *that would work*. Then she would be in and out without him noticing. Whether she found anything noteworthy or not, she would go straight to the detectives then. Reggie sat on her shoulder quietly, his calming influence much appreciated as Flora's heart felt like it was going to beat straight out of her chest. Now, all she had to do was wait.

Half an hour passed, and Flora busied herself wiping down the counter tops. She assumed the detectives were still busy interviewing, but with the age of the house being what it was, the walls were so thick that you couldn't hear between the front of the house and the back. They could have left to drive down to the village for all Flora knew. Still, she had decided on this course of action, and she was committed to it now.

Movement out of the corner of her eye caught Flora's attention. She let out a quick sigh of relief as she saw Mitch, who had come from the far corner of the house and not the side beside the rose garden, and gone straight to his shed.

"It's now or never, Buddy," Flora whispered to Reggie, who stayed on her shoulder as she rushed out of the back door and around the back of the house.

"Mitch!" She shouted as nonchalantly as possible.

"Oh, Flora! You gave me a shock," he stood up suddenly, filling the doorway of the tiny wooden hut.

"Yes, well, I got a shock of my own a moment ago… I just saw Missy coming through the house looking for you and she was on the warpath! The police must've let her in, if I were you I'd make myself scarce for a few minutes!"

"Really? Thanks for the heads up, Flora," he winked, which made Flora feel rather nauseous, then hurried off the way he had come, his shed apparently forgotten. This made Flora wonder whether the man was actually hiding anything in there or not, since he could abandon it so easily, but she hurried forward nonetheless.

The late afternoon sun shone through the tiny windows, causing patches of light, but everything else in the shed remained dark. The place must've spooked Reggie, as he flapped his wings suddenly, causing a crash from the shelf behind him. Flora bent down to see what it was, only to find a pestle and mortar.

"Unusual," Flora whispered to the bird, and went to pick them up before something at the back of her mind stopped her. She quickly removed her thick gloves from her apron pocket and put them on, before handling the items, "just in case."

"I think we may have all we need," Flora whispered to Reggie, stepping out into the sunshine where the bird was waiting.

"And what would that be?" A very male voice spoke ominously behind her.

Not waiting to see, as she knew exactly who it was, Flora took off at a run. Sensing her distress, Reggie divebombed her pursuer, pecking at Mitch's face to give Flora time to get away. She wouldn't make it all the way through to the dining room on her dodgy ankle, she knew that much, so Flora ducked into the study instead, clutching her precious cargo tightly in her gloved hands.

"You didn't think I'd fall for that one, did you?" Flora heard Mitch shout behind her, apparently not at all out of breath. She heard him going down the steps to the laundry and utility room, presumably thinking she would hide there. Flora quickly tucked the wooden items into her apron pocket and yanked the candlestick on the mantle hiding the lever which opened the secret office. Reggie came shooting into the room just as the door slid open, and the pair of them jumped inside, pulling the door shut just as Flora heard Mitch's footsteps coming into the room.

Flora's breaths were coming in short gasps, and she was about to reach into her pocket for her phone to call for help when she remembered two things – that she still had on her gardening gloves, which were potentially contaminated with poisonous Monkshood, and that she had dropped the pestle and mortar into her apron pocket, meaning the inside of that material, and also her phone which nestled there, were potentially covered as well.

"Damn!" Flora scolded herself for her own stupidity, while Reggie listened intently to the man outside the door. He must've seen them go in, as he could be heard scraping along the wall and the bookshelves, looking for the way to open the secret room.

"There's no way out," Flora whispered to the little bird.

"Don't worry, Flora, I can wait here as long as it takes," Mitch's tone was menacing, and Flora felt her eyes well with tears. She tried shouting for help, but all that earned her was an evil laugh from the man on the other side of the door, "They can't hear you, Flora, whoever built that room did a good job of soundproofing it, I can only hear a muffle myself! And no windows, or I'd have noticed them from the outside. I wonder how much air there is in there? It seems pretty self-contained. A bit like an elevator, you'll run out of air if I don't get to you first. So, tell me how to help you, Flora, tell me where the handle is to unlock the door."

"Help! Help!" Reggie repeated back to her, causing the panic in Flora to build even more.

"I won't tell him, even if it kills me, which it might well do. We need a miracle, little friend, a way out," Flora was talking to herself more than to Reggie, though the bird obviously heard her as he jumped from Flora's shoulder and landed on the floor. He started pacing on the thin rug which ran along the opposite wall, to the side of the large, leather desk chair, scratching at it with his claws.

Flora wondered if he was hungry and this was his way of getting attention, "Not now, Reggie, not now," she muttered.

"Now!" the little parrot repeated, flying up and pulling

on a loose strand of Flora's hair that had come out of her bun.

"Ouch!" Flora yelped, "What on…?" Reggie pulled her head down and so, to avoid further pain, Flora knelt on the floor, as that was clearly where he was keen to get her. Again, the bird began scratching and pecking at the thin woven rug, until Flora took the hint and lifted the edge of the material. All she could see was the varnished wood of the floor, and she was about to give up and scold the silly bird, when something metallic caught Flora's eye.

"A bolt!" Flora exclaimed, before clamping her mouth shut. She would need Mitch to think she was still in here if she had any chance of reaching help.

Lifting the rug entirely, Flora was stunned to see a trapdoor built into the floor. A secret escape route!

And she intended to find out where it led.

TWENTY-SIX

Mitch chatted away, while Flora worked silently to free the bolt, covering her hand with the rug in case he heard the squeaking of the metal. She had shrugged out of the large gloves without touching them, flinging them across the room as she did so, so that they wouldn't come into contact with Reggie's feathers.

"You ladies of a certain age are all the same," Mitch vented, his voice dark and bitter, "All gullible. My aunt believed I'd come to make amends. You see, she and my mother were sisters. One married a rich landowner, one a poverty-stricken Italian with an eye for the ladies – I'll let you guess which was which." He let out a short bark of laughter, but there was only pain there, no humour.

When Flora didn't answer he continued, presumably thinking he had all the time in the world while she was captive in the room, "She wouldn't help my mother out when she was trying to raise me single-handedly, wouldn't take me in when she died of an overdose, so I came back last year when I'd got my degree – full bursary because I'd come from the care system – and after I'd had a bit of fun, and told the esteemed Lady Errington that I was a redeemed character, asked her to take me on as the gardener. Did she accept out of a sense of guilt? Possibly. Did I care? Not at all. All I needed was to be close enough to get rid of her, to make her pay," luckily, Flora didn't see the evil smile which graced his lips.

"I'd thought to off them both, but then Uncle Rupert had the idea to force you to sell this place, to have me wear you down from the inside and the idea of inheriting both estates was too tempting. They had no children of their own, you see. When I heard Aunt Lavinia was coming here for that competition, it was like the gods were pouring their favour onto me! The perfect place to get away with it, as so many of the local women disliked her. Being able to claim that I might have been the possible victim was the icing on the cake! So many suspects for the police to interview! When she came outside to see me, and I didn't have to lure my aunt into the kitchen to have the éclair – blessed, I tell you! Blessed! She was whinging about me being your gardener – she didn't know about the plot to push you out, of course – so I, as the dutiful nephew I was, offered her the éclair as a peace offering. The éclair that everyone would see was meant for me, thanks to that stupid Scottish girl! I'd already added the poison, and well, you know the rest. Of course, I'm going to frame my uncle for it eventually, when the police investigation comes up with nothing that'll stick, getting him safely out of the picture. With you suitably disposed of too – you understand, there's no way I can let you go now – I'll be lord of both estates! Perfect plan, perfectly executed! Don't you think? Flora? Flora?"

What the man didn't realise was that Flora was long gone. So keen to brag, to extol his own cunning, Mitch hadn't heard Flora and Reggie pull open the trapdoor, and tiptoe down the narrow concrete steps which led into the large basement under the house.

Flora ran through the basement with Reggie on her shoulder, dodging old furniture and boxes, muffling her dust-induced sneezes and glad that there were a few dirt-covered windows that shone tiny slivers of light into the space. It was enough to help her make her way straight to the trapdoor which Flora knew was in the far wall and led to the outside steps at the back of the house. Thankfully, this bolt slid across much more easily than the one in the secret room, and Flora pushed open the heavy, slanted hatch, feeling the welcome blast of fresh air hit her as she peeked out. Reggie was desperate to get out of the confined space and flew straight up as soon as he could fit through the gap, hovering as he waited for Flora to follow.

Seeing that the path was clear, the shed to the side of her still sitting open, Flora pushed out of the opening, ran up the steps and around the far side of the building, in the direction Mitch had approached from earlier, her heavy apron jiggling as she moved with its potentially precious cargo. This side of the house was darker than the other, and bordered by a thick hedge, though was thankfully free of human life, so Flora ran as fast as she could straight to the dining room window which was the first she reached on this side.

"Help! Come quick!" Flora hammered on the glass, praying that at least one of the two detectives would still be there, "It's Flora!"

Flora's breath came in short, sharp gasps as she peered through the window. The relief which flooded her when she saw McArthur approaching was so immense that Flora's knees almost buckled. She gripped onto the thin window ledge for support.

"Flora?" McArthur asked from the other side of the pane, "Is everything okay?"

"The gardener!" Flora shouted, "It's the gardener!"

"What is?"

"Everything!" Flora saw McArthur's eyes widen, and couldn't hear what she said when she turned her back to the window, but assumed that she had passed the information on to Blackett, as he strode over to join them.

"Don't come to me, go to the study now!" Flora shouted, wondering if at any minute Mitch would come around the corner and find her.

Blackett's eyebrows were drawn so tightly together, they were like a sharp pencil line framing his eyes, "Come inside, Mrs. Miller, please."

McArthur, who had been studying Flora's face closely through the glass, seemed to come to a decision of her own, "Quick Blackett, you head to the study to find the man, and I'll go out the front door to meet Flora. What harm can it do? She seems pretty shaken."

Blackett clearly didn't like the plan, and Flora could see his lips form the shape of a sigh, but he turned on his heel and hurried from the room.

"I'll meet you out front," McArthur said, and she too turned away.

Flora felt so stiff she could barely move. She had gone over on her ankle again and that was throbbing, but not nearly as badly as the pulsating pain of a migraine behind her left temple. Fear. That was what still coursed through her veins, and it was that knowledge that pushed Flora to get her feet moving again. The threat that Mitch might come around from the back of the building at any moment and find her.

Reggie had been perched protectively on Flora's shoulder throughout the whole exchange and, sensing his companion's renewed sense of urgency, he flew on ahead once again. They met up with McArthur in front of the house, and Flora had not been so relieved to see someone since Amy had rescued her earlier in the year.

"I didn't hear the whole confession, I was too busy trying to escape, but it's him. The murder, the crime up here, everything. He's their nephew," Flora was babbling away in her desire to offload it all onto the detective, so her chest could be free of the weight of it, "I have what I think he used to grind the plant roots to make the poison. You'd better not touch it without gloves though, just in case, I couldn't use my phone because of it, but maybe there's no signal in that tiny space anyway…"

"Breathe, Flora, I've got you now," McArthur put her arm around Flora's shoulders and guided her inside the main door.

"Did he come your way?" Blackett shouted, running along the hallway towards them, "he wasn't in the study."

"No, did you send the uniformed officer who was in the sitting room to search?"

"Yes, but this is a big property, he could be hiding anywhere," Blackett was barely containing his fury.

"I'll radio for backup," McArthur said, as Blackett dashed off again, speaking into his own phone, "will you be okay in here, Flora?" She indicated the dining room, in which Flora had never felt comfortable at the best of times.

"Um, well, I…"

"I really must join the search," McArthur was already heading out of the room, and Flora had no choice but to sit down. Her only comfort the little bird perching on the table beside her.

She was alone again. And having some quiet time to herself had never felt worse.

TWENTY-SEVEN

It had been two weeks since everything had kicked off at The Rise. Two weeks in which Mitch D'Alessio had not been found. In which Flora had spent every waking moment afraid to be alone, and every night facing him in her nightmares. The police had tried to reassure her that he was probably long gone, and Adam had spent as much time at the coach house as he could, taking her to his apartment in Morpeth when he needed to be in work, but it wasn't a sustainable plan. Flora had businesses to run, which were being sorely neglected, and a semblance of a normal life to lead. Even Reggie had withdrawn into himself, reflecting Flora's misery.

"Let's set a date. Give us something happy to focus

on," Adam had said one night, when Flora had spent another evening sobbing on him.

She knew what he was doing, of course, trying to give her a project to take her mind off things. But she didn't want their wedding day to be a 'project' and she didn't know how she would ever stop re-hashing every second of that day in the big house in her mind. At least, not while Mitch was still out there somewhere. She had been well scolded by the police, Blackett in particular, for going out on a limb by herself again and not coming straight to them with her suspicions. When Mitch's room had been searched they had found detailed plans of both The Rise and The Withers, plans which joined both estates into one huge expanse. More worrying still, though, were the books on 'UK's deadliest plants' and suchlike. Flora shuddered at the thought.

"Not yet," she had whispered, succumbing to tears once again, and Adam had shaken his head slightly, the same pained look on his face that he had worn since she'd told him what had happened.

"I can't bear it, seeing you like this," Adam scrubbed his hand through his hair, "there must be something they've missed up at the big house, when they searched his room, or even over at The Withers."

"Well, how would I know if they've missed something?" Flora snapped, then instantly regretted it. She had been quick to fly off the handle lately, probably from the stress and lack of sleep, not that she thought that was an excuse, "I'm sorry, I'm so sorry for all of it."

"Hey, it's not your fault. None of it," Adam held her closer, "let me think on it some more."

"Tell me again what you heard the man say while you were trapped in the secret office," Adam asked gently the next day.

"Really, Adam, I'd rather not go through it all again. As I've said, I was more focused on getting the trapdoor in the floor open than listening to his homicidal bragging."

"Humour me, love, just tell me the first bit."

"Okay," Flora let out a long sigh before continuing, "well he said that all the women he knew of a certain age – his aunt, me, I guess Missy Christie would also fall into that – were gullible. Basically, he was saying he had played us like fools. Do you need to hear the rest?"

"No, no that's perfect. It's given me an idea that might just work. Can you organise another gathering of the ladies from the two villages? The ones who were there for the competition?"

"I'd rather not go up to the big house at the moment," Flora hadn't been back since that day.

"In the tearoom then, the venue isn't important."

"Perhaps, I mean Phoebe won't be there as she's already gone back to Scotland with Lachlan, but I could ask the others... what do you have in mind?"

"Do you have someone who isn't subtle, but who could keep a secret?"

"There are a few of my friends who fit that bill, yes," Flora gave a small half-smile as she thought fondly of the friendships she had made since coming to Baker's Rise.

"Perfect. Let me speak to Blackett and McArthur and then I'll explain..."

And so it was that the following Saturday Flora found herself hosting another gathering for the local ladies of the W.I. Betty had come this time, as Harry was now out of hospital and had been recovering well at home, but other than that everyone that made it to the impromptu afternoon tea had been present at the choux competition. Flora had spread the word that the event was to make up for the awful time they had shared at the big house and, more importantly, to honour Lavinia's memory. Each lady had baked her favourite recipe to bring along, and Reggie had been warned to be on his best behaviour. Not that Flora expected anything but the quiet, docile bird she had shared her home with this past couple of weeks. Even Will had commented on the change in Reggie's character when he had visited with Shona and Aaron to see how Flora was doing. Poor Reggie's melancholy had caused his appetite to reduce, and Flora had had trouble tempting him even with fruit salads – normally his favourite. The vet had remarked on the bird's weight loss, saying that the diet had clearly worked but Flora must make sure the reduced eating didn't continue for too long. This had only added to Flora's worries, and she regarded her little friend with concern now, as Tanya and Lily busied themselves arranging the plates of cakes and buns.

A few eyebrows were raised when Missy Christie arrived wearing what could only be described as a thigh-length silk robe, the tops of her stockings visible at the hem.

"Is that lingerie?" Tanya asked Flora in a stage whisper, as Betty and Hilda May tut-tutted their disapproval from the corner of the big table.

"I think it's meant to be a dress," Amy replied, balancing a tray on her tiny baby bump, and always the first to see the best in everyone.

When all were settled with cups of tea and plates of cake and sandwiches, Flora gave a knowing nod to Lily, who spoke up loudly, "So, Flora, I hear you may be on the lookout for a new gardener. My godson, Laurie, would love to offer his services for the role. I'm sure he'll be a much better fit for you."

"Of course," Flora replied, following their rehearsed conversation, "You never did tell me why he disliked Mitch so much."

"Well, there's a sordid story there, to be sure. You know what a womaniser that man was. Well, he went one step further with poor Laurie's girlfriend at university, who succumbed to his expert seduction techniques and ended up pregnant."

"No! I'm guessing the rogue didn't stand by her," Flora replied, watching Missy's reaction from the corner of her eye. The whole table had hushed now, as all the ladies listened in.

"Of course not," Lily shook her head in disgust.

"Not that I'm surprised, from what he confessed to me when he had me trapped, Mitch D'Alessio thinks all women are gullible and only exist to be played by him," Flora said loudly.

"Men like that, no loyalty," Tanya chimed in, "always sniffing around for the next skirt."

"He used my Phoebe something rotten," Jean added sadly, "just to ingratiate himself into village life, I think. Used her, then threw her away like an old rag. The silly girl fell for his charm like so many others, it seems."

There was a loud scrape as Missy Christie pushed her chair back from the table.

"Are you okay, Missy?" Flora asked, allowing a small flash of victory to warm her insides.

"I, I, ah, headache. Migraine come on suddenly," Missy muttered, clutching her palm to her face.

"Fancy that," Tanya said wryly, as Missy made a hasty exit, all eyes on her retreating back.

"We're on," Flora texted Adam from the phone she had kept in her pocket.

As they heard Missy's car skid along the gravel driveway, Flora knew that the well-placed, unmarked police cars would track her, either back to her home in the centre of Witherham village, Ibeza Cottage, or to wherever else she was helping Mitch to remain undetected. For surely, she was going to have words with her 'fiancé,' of that Flora had no doubt.

TWENTY-EIGHT

The next day dawned warm and bright, and Flora awoke with a lightness of spirit and a feeling of hope that she had not felt in a long while. Blackett's hunch that Missy was harbouring the murderer, but which he had been unable to get her to confess to, had been proven correct thanks to Adam's plan and the ladies' ruse. Mitch was now safely behind bars, and Flora was content that he couldn't reach her now. There had been truth in her conversation with Lily, though, as Laurie was going to be her new live-in gardener at The Rise, and he would be moving in with his wife and their two-year old son – Mitch's biological child – as Laurie had been in love with Rosa despite her brief fling with the other man and they had been a family since he had

R. A. Hutchins

looked after her throughout her unexpected pregnancy. Their story warmed Flora's heart, and proved there were still plenty of good men out there.

Her own Adam was another fine example, and Flora checked her hair and lipstick quickly in the mirror as she awaited her fiancé to walk with her to church. Today was the much anticipated pet service, and Reggie was coming in his little bird carrier. As if sensing her relief yesterday evening, the parrot had managed to guzzle down a banana, five grapes and a bowlful of seed, whilst chirping, "My Flora" happily. Flora was thrilled to have his personality shining through again, but slightly concerned that it might shine rather too brightly in the church service!

"All set, love?" Adam kissed her on the lips by way of greeting as Flora locked the door to the coach house.

"Yes, perfect actually," Flora smiled widely, linking arms and setting a fast pace so they could meet Harry and Betty on the walk to church.

Other than the addition of a walking cane, Harry was back to his usual self and Flora was glad of it. The world felt as if it was back on its right axis again in the little village of Baker's Rise as the villagers gathered with a veritable ark full of pets – furry, feathered, shelled and scaly.

Reverend Marshall stood welcoming them all into the building as usual and, at the request of his daughters, Flora had already let Reggie out of the case to sit freely on her shoulder. He and Tina the terrier had had their usual screeching-barking moment of recognition, which Flora hoped had got the excitement out of her little bird's system.

"Good morning, Flora, Adam, and is this Reggie I spy?" The vicar chuckled and leant in to stroke Reggie.

"You sexy beast!" Reggie replied, squawking for all assembled to hear.

"Well, I think he's, er, found his voice again," Flora mumbled, slightly mortified, until she saw the laughter in the reverend's eyes. It moved from there to his chest which started shaking with the force of his amusement. Soon everyone was laughing, and Reggie, happy to be the centre of attention, played up to the role by giving them a full rendition of his most embarrassing vocabulary – much to Flora's initial dismay, though she was soon chuckling along with everyone else, her embarrassment forgotten.

Some things never change, Flora thought, *and nor would I want them to.*

R. A. Hutchins

Join Flora and Reggie in **"All's Fair in Loaf and War,"** *the next instalment in the Baker's Rise Mysteries series, to see whether Flora and Adam manage to tie the knot!*

All's Fair in Loaf and War

Baker's Rise Mysteries Book Six

Publication Date July 1st 2022

The much-anticipated sixth story in the Baker's Rise Mysteries series brings more of the cosy humour and quaint village life which make Baker's Rise such a special place to visit!

Wedding preparations are well underway at The Rise, and there is a growing sense of excitement about the place.

Frustrated at not being the centre of attention, Reggie starts sticking his beak where it's not wanted. As things start to go missing, could he really be the culprit?

When Flora makes the choice to hire wedding caterers, Reggie isn't the only one whose beak is out of joint around the place! Will it be tiers or tears where the wedding cake is concerned?

Packed with twists and turns, colourful characters and more than a sprinkle of romance, this new mystery will certainly leave you hungry for more!

R. A. Hutchins

Fresh as a Daisy

The Lillymouth Mysteries Book One

Coming Summer 2022

Keep your eyes peeled for a brand new series coming to Amazon later this year!

Featuring a new lady vicar, a grumpy vicarage cat, and a seaside town in Yorkshire full of hidden secrets and more than a mystery or two!

R. A. Hutchins

ABOUT THE AUTHOR

Rachel Hutchins lives in northeast England with her husband, three children and their dog Boudicca. She loves writing both mysteries and romances, and enjoys reading these genres too! Her favourite place is walking along the local coastline, with a coffee and some cake!

You can connect with Rachel and sign up to her monthly **newsletter** via her website at:

www.authorrachelhutchins.com

Alternatively, she has social media pages on:

Facebook: www.facebook.com/rahutchinsauthor

Instagram: www.instagram.com/ra_hutchins_author

R. A. Hutchins

OTHER BOOKS BY R. A. HUTCHINS

"The Angel and the Wolf"

What do a beautiful recluse, a well-trained husky, and a middle-aged biker have in common?
Find out in this poignant story of love and hope!

When Isaac meets the Angel and her Wolf, he's unsure whether he's in Hell or Heaven.
Worse still, he can't remember taking that final step.
They say that calm follows the storm, but will that be the case for Isaac?

Fate has led him to her door,
Will she have the courage to let him in?

"To Catch A Feather" (Found in Fife Book One)

When tragedy strikes an already vulnerable Kate Winters, she retreats into herself, broken and beaten. Existing rather than living, she makes a journey North to try to find herself, or maybe just looking for some sort of closure.

Cameron McAllister has known his own share of grief and love lost. His son, Josh, is now his only priority. In his forties and running a small coffee shop in a tiny Scottish fishing village, Cal knows he is unlikely to find love again.

When the two meet and sparks fly, can they overcome their past losses and move on towards a shared future, or are the memories which haunt them still too real?

These books, as well as others by Rachel, can be found on Amazon worldwide in e-book and paperback formats, as well as free to read on Kindle Unlimited.

Printed in Great Britain
by Amazon